The
KAYA GIRL

Mamle Wolo

LITTLE, BROWN AND COMPANY
New York Boston

Little, Brown and Company
Hachette Book Group
1290 Avenue of the Americas, New York, NY 10104
Visit us at LBYR.com

First Edition: June 2022

Little, Brown and Company is a division of Hachette Book Group, Inc. The Little, Brown name and logo are trademarks of Hachette Book Group, Inc.

The publisher is not responsible for websites (or their content) that are not owned by the publisher.

Library of Congress Cataloging-in-Publication Data
Names: Wolo, Mamle, author.
Title: The kaya girl / Mamle Wolo.
Description: First edition. | New York ; Boston : Little, Brown and Company, 2022. | "Adapted from The Kaya-Girl, originally published in Ghana in 2012 by Techmate Publishers Ltd and in 2018 by Nsona Books." | Audience: Ages 8-12. | Summary: "Fourteen-year-olds Abena and Faiza, girls from vastly different social worlds, cross paths in hectic Makola Market in Accra, Ghana, and forge a beautiful bond that changes the path of each of their lives."—Provided by publisher.
Identifiers: LCCN 2021021213 | ISBN 9780316703932 (hardcover) | ISBN 9780316703925 (ebook)
Subjects: CYAC: Friendship—Fiction. | Markets—Fiction. | Social classes—Fiction. | Family life—Fiction. | Ghana—Fiction. | LCGFT: Novels.
Classification: LCC PZ7.W83655 Kay 2022 | DDC [Fic]—dc23
LC record available at https://lccn.loc.gov/2021021213

ISBNs: 978-0-316-70393-2 (hardcover), 978-0-316-70392-5 (ebook)

Printed in the United States of America

LSC-C

Printing 1, 2022

For my children,
Karl and Kristin

And for the work of
School for Life, Ghana,
and all other champions
of second-chance
education for children

GHANA

PART ONE

Chapter 1

ORANGE HEADSCARF, KOHL-LINED EYES, HIGH-UP CHEEKS, BRIGHT white teeth. She walked into the frame as I was taking a photo out the car window.

Auntie Lydia was just pulling into our usual spot at the market car park, and the girl came and lowered her head pan by the car next to us: a great silver bowl full of Blankson's Electricals carrier bags, with their unmistakable green-and-blue logo. The very sight of that logo made the Blankson boys pop up before my eyes like genies from a bottle.

"Are you waiting for angels to come and carry you out of the car?" snapped Auntie, blowing my vision away like a puff of smoke.

She flicked a glossy curl into place in the rearview mirror. After a week with her, I was growing a tougher skin against her sharp tongue. I noticed suddenly how stuffy it was now that we were parked. Life without air-conditioning sure took some getting used to. And this was June. I couldn't even imagine this life in the hot season.

Gifty and I opened our doors in unison—mine at the front, hers at the back—and stepped out into the pungent dustiness of the car park. I wiped sweat off my forehead, unstuck my clammy skirt behind me, and slammed my door. Another hectic day in Makola Market.

As we unloaded Auntie's goods from the trunk, the porter girl looked over at us, a bag dangling from either hand.

Gifty was staring, and I could see she was hoping Auntie would call the girl to carry our bags to the shop.

"It's all your fault, Abena," she hissed as we trotted, loaded down, behind Auntie, weaving our way between vegetable stalls. "Now there's two of us, she thinks we can carry everything ourselves." She freed a hand to drape her three loose braids carefully across her forehead and tuck them behind one ear, walking lopsided for a moment with two bags in one hand.

"Don't worry, I won't be around for long."

I felt as if I were trying to convince myself. The truth was, the long vacation stretched out endlessly before me. I looked around once again at this place I had landed myself in. The colors made me think of the flag—tomatoes for red, garden eggs for yellow, okros for green, all piled high on tables tended by women in massive-brimmed straw hats. Red, gold, green: Ghana.

"Why did you snap that girl, anyway?"

"For my school project."

She grunted, bored already.

It wasn't really a school project. I had entered an online "junior journalists" competition for high schoolers. It was a long shot, but it seemed like a fun thing to do, and I thought it might help get me through this summer holiday. In fact, it was one of the reasons I'd agreed to come and help out in Auntie Lydia's shop. Makola was teeming with opportunities for an article. And if, by some miracle, I placed in the competition, who knew, it just might help me become a journalist one day. But I wasn't going to discuss that with Gifty. Or anyone, really. Not now, anyway.

I turned around and walked backward for a few paces to take discreet photos of the crowd. A human wave of color and energy, rolling toward me. *Market Vista*. That would make a cool tag. The girl was back there somewhere, orange headscarf bobbing up and down.

When we got to the shop, I flicked quickly through my photos. I'd been getting carried away and needed to free up space on my phone. I scrolled to the one of her. *Porter Girl*, I thought, or *Kayayoo*. But she wasn't even fully in focus because I'd meant to get a shot of the car park when I took it. My finger hovered over the delete button. Something in her face held me back.

An intensity.

That was it, I thought, seeing it again a few hours later. It was uncanny how soon our paths had crossed again given the size of the market. Auntie had sent me to call a porter for a customer, and as soon as I stepped out of the shop, there she was.

"Hi!" I said.

No reply.

"Ɛte sɛn?" I tried again, in Twi this time.

Still she was quiet. She looked frustrated with herself for not being able to reply. But she lowered her head pan with a shy smile that did the talking for her. It said she recognized me too, and that she didn't mean to be rude. I smiled back, and suddenly language did not seem important. It was as if we knew each other already.

"Abena, stop wasting time and bring her inside," my aunt called from inside the shop, "She is here to carry things, not to chat with you. Hey, small girl, bra!" she finished off brusquely, ordering the girl inside with a curl of her fingers.

She hurried in carrying her oversize bowl before her and placed it at Auntie Lydia's feet. As she bent down, I could see that her eye was caught by the gleaming French manicure on Auntie's long, pointy toenails. Eyes still lowered, she collected six bulging carrier bags from the plump customer with eight rings on her fingers. The woman must have owned a sewing shop or something, because there were more than twenty pieces of wax print in there, their bold motifs peeking out at the tops of the bags. A bunch of lining fabrics too, in sateen and polyester. I smiled to myself—I was already becoming a textiles expert.

The girl tried to pack them into her head pan, but the overstuffed bags seemed to jostle each other, and bulged precariously over the rim. The woman was still chatting to Auntie, so the girl quietly removed the cloths from their bags, used the bags to line the bottom of the bowl, and arranged the rolls of fabric deftly inside. I wished I could photograph her doing it, but that would be weird, and my phone was in Auntie's desk drawer, anyway. I wasn't supposed to use it while serving customers. One of her many rules.

It was a shame because she had actually created a pattern inside the bowl: a rainbow kaleidoscope of African print interspersed with plain blocks of contrast from the lining fabrics. She wedged in the last cloth and paused. This was the awkward moment because she needed help but did not know how to ask for it. I rushed over and grabbed the rim of the bowl to help lift it onto her head. We struggled a bit as it tipped precariously in my direction. Then it was up, sitting snugly on the flattened pad on her head, a faded scarf rolled into a cloth snail shell.

As we did this, a new customer entered the shop, immaculate in a white lace Anago wrapper and top with a red-and-gold gele on her head. It was so gorgeously folded and tied that I resolved then and there to go to the shop next door and beg the Nigerian lady to teach me how to do it. Auntie was mesmerized too, so I took advantage and slipped out, following the girl with the huge bowl on her head.

I could not believe how straight and fast she walked. I pictured what would have happened if it had been me instead, balancing that weight! I was sturdier and a whole head taller, but I felt like my neck would have been pushed down into my chest, and my knees would have collapsed into my feet. We walked in single file: Auntie's customer, who had now become the girl's, leading the way toward her car; the girl following; and me, unseen, bringing up the rear. Rain clouds were slowly darkening the sky, and I did not really know why I was following.

Maybe I was already getting bored spending all day every day at Auntie's shop. The evenings weren't much better. She didn't even have cable at her place, let alone Wi-Fi. So far, I was just living for my weekends back home, but it wasn't the same without Mom. I wished she hadn't gone all the way to London to have my baby brother. Dad was still here, but it didn't make much difference because he could barely get away from the clinic these days. The new wing had just opened, plus he'd started teaching at the medical school.

When Auntie Lydia had offered to have me for the summer holidays, I hadn't been keen. She was Mom's sister, though you'd never have guessed it. She was much older, and they hadn't grown up together because they had different moms. So we never saw as much of her as we did of Auntie Adjoa and Uncle Frank, even though they didn't even live in Ghana anymore.

I was a bit scared of Auntie Lydia, but it would have been rude to say no. She was...kind of unnerving. Her resting face was annoyed, and she had bleached it lighter than the rest of her body, making the hairs on her upper lip stand out like a faint mustache. Her laughter was a sudden boom that transformed her into the most tickled person on earth, but the moment it ended there was no believing she was the same woman.

I suspected Mom was a bit nervous about the whole idea too. But Auntie Lydia was so excited, and Dad said the change would do me good and give me a taste of real Ghana life at last. I wasn't sure I liked the sound of that. I knew why he'd said it, though. He'd wanted me to go to a Ghanaian boarding school for high school, and Mom had vetoed it in favor of the American School.

At first, I begged them to give Auntie some excuse, but then I thought how boring it would be at home on my own. My school friends were all going abroad. That was the problem with international schools. Mind you, my Ghanaian schoolmates were traveling too. My best buddy, Lucy, wasn't even coming back after the holidays. She was Tanzanian, and her father worked for the United Nations, and they were moving to India next, but she was going back home for the holidays first. I never heard much from her when she was back in Tanzania, because she was so busy catching up with her old friends there.

So I felt kind of at loose ends, but also, to be honest, part of me was curious. Even before I'd made up my mind about the junior journalists thing. A brave kind of curious. My friends thought I was bluffing—*Seriously? Your aunt's shop in Makola Market?* This was going to be different from anything I'd ever done in my life.

Mom hardly ever went to the market. She said it exhausted her, so she sent our house help, Dinah, every week instead. I'd only been to Makola the couple of times she went to visit Auntie Lydia there. It wasn't the kind of place I'd hang with my besties. When we wanted to buy clothes and other stuff, we went to Accra Mall or West Hills Mall or the boutiques in Osu.

But Makola was fascinating—all the hustle and bustle, the smells and the colors. And I knew you could get stuff there for a fraction of what it cost in Osu. Plus, you could haggle it even lower. It seemed like you could find anything in the world if you just looked hard enough. One minute you'd be admiring sequined lace fabric, and the next, you'd almost stumble over a tray of coiling, writhing black snails. You'd see groundnut paste in huge bowls, enough to dive into, and substances you never knew existed—rolled into balls, cut into blocks, twisted into shapes—that you wondered how on earth you were meant to use. As food? Soap for a bath? Bricks for a house?

It just had this feel of a place where anything could happen. Maybe Mom was right; maybe my imagination was always in overdrive. I knew Makola was just a smelly, chaotic place to her. But to me it seemed like one where you could trip over something and find yourself in a different world when you got up.

The problem was, working at the shop didn't give me much chance to explore. And Auntie didn't like me wandering off on my own. She seemed to see me as some pampered Rapunzel she had to protect from the outside world. I liked the shop, but I was starting to get cabin fever. Her stuffy little house in Abeka Lapaz didn't help—gaudy furniture and knickknacks in gloomy rooms with peeling paint, and everything covered in a film of dust.

I felt homesick in the beginning, especially for

Mom. But at the same time, I was glad she couldn't see me now, because she'd have taken me back home, and I liked the feeling of learning to cope. Dinah could have got the place into some kind of shape, but the best Auntie had was Gifty. With the low tin roof, the heat overpowered the few fans that worked, and the taps were not even running half the time. We had to scoop water from buckets for everything, even for bathing.

But as for her shop, it was one of the fanciest in Makola Market—or so she believed, anyway—with its tiled floor, air-conditioning, and brocade curtains. Stepping inside was like diving into a blaze of color, in the boldest shades and patterns. Racks and stands in the middle were draped and stacked with cloth, and folded pieces were piled high on shelves at either side. African print was her main merchandise, though the bulk of her brands were made in China, with a few from Ghana. Her English and Dutch wax prints were in glass cabinets that we needed the stepladder to reach. She also stocked locally made batiks and a general range of imported fabrics—print, lace, velvet, and sateen from all over the world. Then there was what she termed her "heritage" collection: indigo from Nigeria, mud cloth from Mali, our own kente cloth, and other traditional African textiles.

In addition, she sold plain lining materials in every conceivable shade, and rolls and rolls of trimmings—lacy, embroidered, diamanté-encrusted. A standing glass cabinet contained costume jewelry, also glittering with rhinestones in every hue. And as if there weren't enough color already, the walls were covered with posters of curvy women in gorgeous outfits—mostly the matching fitted top and skirt, full-length and fishtail, of the traditional kaba and slit, tailored in the latest styles from African print.

We half lived in the shop, so it wasn't all for the customers. Auntie's desk was by the entrance, but we had our own private space at the back too. She'd fenced it off with two ornate screens covered in yellow-and-violet African print. A slight overlap between them led to the customer-free zone. On one side was an old fridge with a microwave oven on top, and a worktable with a manual sewing machine. On the other was a threadbare old set of furniture, including a sagging sofa on which she often catnapped. A small door led to an added-on cubicle partitioned with a cramped toilet and sink on the left and a tiny storeroom on the right.

It was not called Lydia's Palace for nothing, because when she got ready in the mornings, Auntie Lydia looked like a queen. Oh, she was a proper market queen, my auntie. She applied her heavy face powder in a shade light enough for her face, penciled over her razor-trimmed eyebrows, outlined her lips with the same black liner, and filled in lipstick in shades of red, fuchsia, or purple. She tidied up her curly weave and sprayed something in to make it shine. Then she put on a kaba and slit, usually made from the latest print in the shop. She topped this off by tying the matching cover cloth into an imposing headdress.

The one thing that disappointed me about the shop, though, was that it had no cash till. I had always longed to press the buttons on those machines like the uniformed shop assistants sitting in rows in the supermarkets, tapping their fingers so fast and so expertly over the keys. No, Auntie just collected all the money—rather untidily, I thought—in the lower drawer of her desk. But it was still exciting to see all the pretty things in the shop and to be given the responsibility of serving customers. It made me feel quite grown up.

❖

Although I'd noticed the girls with large head pans walking around on my first day, I hadn't paid them much attention till one came into the shop. That was when a customer had made a large purchase.

"Abena, go outside and call us a kayayoo," Auntie said.

"A kaya-what?"

"Hmm, your parents are making a broni out of you at that American School." Auntie smiled, glancing with a mixture of pride and embarrassment at her customers.

Being the niece from the most expensive high school in Ghana was no problem. In fact, I'd soon realized it was the main reason she'd wanted me in her shop. Having someone who "sounded expensive"—her description of me—serve the customers was exactly what she wanted. But sounding like a broni—a white person, or what she really meant, a clueless foreigner—was taking the glamour too far, even for her. Gifty called me broni too, though I was darker-skinned than she was, to show that she didn't consider someone as privileged as me a real Ghanaian.

"You don't know kayayei? Those girls walking all over the market with pans on their heads?"

"Oh, them!"

"Kɔ pɛ bi ma me!" She switched to Twi in that deliberate manner she used when she was on a mission to rescue the Ghanaian in me. "Go find me one!"

I stepped outside, blinking in the blazing sunshine, and screwed up my eyes, trying to spot one of the girls Auntie was talking about. It didn't take long, because the girl signaled pertly when she saw me scanning the stalls and alleys. I nodded, and she marched briskly to the shop.

I'd noticed them more since then, but I'd never had the urge to talk to them until today.

This one was different. She looked no older than me, and behind her intensity, there was a shy, slightly scared look in her eyes. And when I realized she didn't speak any language I knew, I was amazed and intrigued. A girl working as a market porter might not know English, because she wasn't going to school. But how could she possibly manage in Makola Market without Twi or Ga?

What did she speak, I wondered as I trailed her and her customer. Perhaps I'd find out when we reached the car park.

But I did not. She just lowered her head pan, packed the rolls of cloth back into their bags, and placed them in the madam's car trunk for her. Then she accepted the proffered coins with a tiny nod and lifted the empty bowl back onto her head. The car sparked with a rich purr as she turned around. She saw me immediately, and I knew she was not surprised, although she'd had no idea I was following her. She smiled the same smile. It was the second time, and I noticed the same thing, that when she smiled at me, the lost look in her eyes disappeared. Perhaps that was what had made me follow her.

The wind was stirring up dust, and vendors around the car park were starting to pack away their wares. Rain seemed certain, but you could never tell at this time of year whether it would actually fall or blow over. I didn't want to get caught in a downpour, and I knew Auntie would be wondering where I was. Judging from the girl's grip on her bowl, she knew she should be looking for her next customer. But she just walked over to me

17

as if we had an appointment. We looked at each other, and I noticed she had a fine line etched vertically in the middle of each cheek.

"Yɛfrɛ me Abena," I said in Twi, putting a hand up to my chest.

"N yuli Faiza," she said in a language I would soon find out was called Dagbanli.

We did not speak each other's languages, but I heard her name and she heard mine. And I found out other things about her too, that day. Don't ask me how, but she was just so easy to talk to. There was a calmness about her that made it seem as if we had all the time in the world, even while the wind whipped around us. I spoke a bit more Twi, and she spoke a bit more Dagbanli, and I guess we must have used some sign language and a few universal words that she could understand as we stood there amid people dashing for shelter, barely noticing the few drops the clouds flecked us with as they moved lazily on.

In our patchwork of communication there was laughter, and exclamations, and no one watching from a distance could have dreamed we had no language in common. It was like speaking made-up language with a baby; the words didn't matter because the meaning was in everything else—the intonation, the eye contact, the body language. I don't know how to explain it, but I found her easier to talk to than people with whom I could converse in two or three languages. She came from a place called Tolon, in the Northern Region, and she had just arrived in Accra the day before.

And she was fourteen years old, like me.

Chapter 2

WHEN I GOT BACK TO AUNTIE'S SHOP, IT WAS LIKE MAGIC WEAR-
ing off. Auntie Lydia just had a way of squeezing it out
of things, like wringing water from a rag. Faiza became
nothing but a kayayoo once again.

Auntie didn't know whether to be amused or
annoyed that I knew her name. "You followed that
kayayoo to the car park?"

I hadn't had time to make up a better story, so I told
her I'd been worried she might drop our goods because
they were so heavy.

"Those girls drop something?" she sneered. "Their
neck muscles are made of steel. You don't know the
things they carry up there where they come from."

Gifty sniggered, sweeping the floor. She was Auntie's niece by marriage, the daughter of one of her husband's many poor relatives, from a village somewhere in the Eastern Region. Even Auntie didn't seem to know much about her family, and Gifty was sullen whenever I tried to ask about it.

I couldn't figure out if Auntie was still with her husband, because I never saw him. Whatever the case, Gifty lived with her the same way my cousin Koshie had lived with us before she got to senior high and Dad sent her to Holy Child in Cape Coast, the kind of girls' boarding school he would have liked me to attend. Gifty helped Auntie at home and in the shop, and she was doing a part-time apprenticeship with a seamstress in the market.

Gifty laughed. "Hausa girl from North!" she said, pronouncing it "Nof."

"Yɛ komm!" barked Auntie Lydia. "Get back to work, you lazy girl."

I felt bad when Auntie talked to her like that, because she treated me differently, and yet, in a broad kind of way, we were all family. Not that I particularly liked Gifty. The only thing she had in common with Koshie was that they'd both been sent to live with relatives because their families were poor.

"And you"—Auntie turned to me—"make yourself useful and get on the computer and check that email account you set up for me."

Yes, madam, I said in my head. I wanted to ask what the kayayoo girls, or whatever they were called, carried where they came from, but she'd find the question cheeky no matter how I put it, and anyway, I had a feeling she wouldn't be interested in going into it. Moreover, I didn't want to give Gifty the satisfaction of sniggering at them again.

I also needed to get back in Auntie's good books after wandering off like that. Helping her with email was the best way. It was the other reason she'd wanted me over the holidays—not just for email but for the computer in general. She was kind of scared of it, but hell-bent on mastering it for her sales. It meant I could use it for myself too, especially for my "school project." Mom had promised to buy me my own laptop in London, and I couldn't wait. I was giving Auntie lessons every day, and I admired her determination, though it took every ounce of my patience. But the laughs were worth it. Her face when she made a mistake...like she was bracing herself for an explosion.

I sat at the desk, and she asked me to read out her emails as she took new fabrics out of the bags we had brought along in the morning and draped them over the racks. Gifty packed away the broom and dustpan in the storeroom and left for her sewing class. Auntie wanted her to help with the shop display, and Gifty was beginning to stitch fabrics from the shop into rudimentary garments to drape over the mannequin in the window, a pale creature with an auburn wig who looked a bit freaked out in baggy African print.

I enjoyed the break from Gifty, and I liked watching Auntie at work. Her fingers were fat, but they moved so nimbly with their sharp, pointy nails, and she handled the fabrics with all the gentleness that was missing from the way she was with people. She stroked down the pile of a blue velvet to even out its sheen, then billowed out a violet chiffon.

I imagined it as the sail of a ship on a sparkling sea. And the gold lurex netting on the next rack, the veil of a pensive princess sitting cross-legged on the deck (on a large blue velvet cushion). The vision came into sharper focus, and suddenly it was me on that ship. Where was I going? To a faraway kingdom to marry a handsome prince, no doubt. That was what princesses did. But... what if this one wanted to sail the seven seas in search of adventure?

"So?" Auntie was staring at me.

"Huh?"

"Did you stop for a chat with a ghost?"

"Er... your emails are done, Auntie."

It was starting to get dark, but only because the storm was on the prowl again. It was not quite five, but Auntie told me to shut down the computer, and she started closing up for the day. As soon as Gifty got back, Auntie said, "Let's get out before the rain beats us o!" She brushed past my elbow to gather up the day's takings from her cash drawer. I slung the laptop bag over my shoulder, and Gifty picked up the empty food Thermos. I didn't relish Auntie's driving or her car at the best of times, and I was in no hurry to try them out in a thunderstorm. The drizzle began as we neared the car park, and we sprinted the rest of the way.

Traffic was bad even though we'd left early. Rain just seemed to do something to people, and they honked and gridlocked their cars worse than ever in the jammed Makola streets as water fell in sheets, blurring everything around us. With no air-conditioning, we were forced to crack open the windows, but it was not enough. It grew stuffy, and we inched toward the middle of the car as water trickled steadily in. The windows and windshield were rapidly steaming up. I pressed the defogger button.

"It doesn't work." Auntie rubbed at the windshield with a duster, but that didn't help either. I looked through the glass. I could see nothing. I took the duster from her and rubbed harder. No difference. I shut my eyes in a moment of panic as the car moved forward. Auntie slammed on the brakes, and there was a screech as the car behind us did the same. If the roar of the rain hadn't drowned out everything, we would have heard its occupants cursing. Auntie was cursing too.

"Gifty, get down and wipe it from outside. Abena, pass her the umbrella, quick!"

"I'll do it!" I hopped out before she could stop me and was drenched before I could even attempt to open the bedraggled umbrella. It got halfway up and the wind tore at it and the rain pounded on it like a sworn enemy.

I snapped it shut and scrubbed at the windshield on Auntie's side with the sopping duster. It felt like cleaning a window in the middle of a waterfall, and I couldn't help smiling.

The world lit up for a second, and thunder crashed into my ears as if it would bring down the sky in fragments around them. I pictured what I must have looked like right then, out on the road, wiping the windshield of a car with no AC and no defogger in a thunderstorm in the middle of Makola Market. Then I pictured my parents watching, and I laughed out loud.

"You this girl!" Auntie said as I flopped back inside, soaking everything around me. "I told you to let Gifty do it. Are you okay?"

"Yes, Auntie."

I grinned to myself. I wouldn't have missed that.

✤

When we got to the house, I changed quickly out of my wet clothes and came to the kitchen, impatient to get through the evening rituals. Auntie never asked me to help with the cooking. She gave orders to Gifty and did some tasks herself, but that only made me uncomfortable because it didn't feel right watching TV or going to my room while they were in the kitchen, sweating over our food. "Don't let your mother go and say I brought you here to be a house girl o!" she'd said when I first offered to help.

I knew she thought I'd only get in the way. And of course I'd rather have curled up on my bed with a book or my diary than sweated in that dingy, smoked-up kitchen, with its patchy linoleum and algae-lined sink. The gas cooker was an ancient thing whose burners rose through ridges of grime. Only two of them worked, and they were lit with actual matches. I was always scared to go in there alone because it felt like anything could jump out at me. I could swear I'd heard squeaks, and I'd seen cockroaches more than once, scuttling away when the light went on. They were fat and glossy, and nothing delighted Gifty more than to watch me lose every shred of my dignity over them.

At first, Auntie only asked me to chop vegetables while Gifty did real stuff like peel and fry yams and plantains, grind up chili peppers, and make banku. I watched her dissolve the fermented corn dough in water, add a bit of cassava dough, and stir it on the stove till it started to thicken. Then she grasped the wooden banku stick like an oar and plowed it through the setting mass.

Chopping veggies looked a bit tame beside all that. I didn't particularly like banku, but I'd signed up for this, and I wasn't going to give them any excuse to call me broni again. Plus, I couldn't help smiling whenever I thought of Dad. How priceless would it be to churn up some banku for him one day? At home, it had never even occurred to me to try to cook. Pierre, our professional chef from Côte d'Ivoire, would have died laughing if I'd asked to help out in the kitchen. But tonight I said, "Let me do the rice, please, Auntie."

She paused, scissor blades hovering over the corner of the rice packet. Gifty looked up from deboning smoked mackerel, holding a spine and tail in midair.

"You want to boil rice?" asked Auntie.

I nodded. How hard could it be?

They both smiled.

"Have you done it before?"

I shook my head, avoiding both sets of eyes.

"Okay. Well...maybe it's time you learned. Two cups of water per cup of rice. Throw in some salt."

Auntie's phone rang, and she stepped out of the kitchen. I measured out the rice and water and threw in some coarse grains of sea salt. I heard her laughter from the living room. It sounded like she was talking to her daughter in America. I didn't really think of her as my cousin, since I'd never met her. All Auntie's children were much older than me.

I struck a match and held it nervously to the burner, backing away as it whooshed into flame. I set the pan on the stove. She came back with the phone held to one ear and lifted the lid with her other hand.

"Oh!" she studied the cloudy froth. "Pat, me srɛ wo, hold on," she said into the phone. And to me, "You didn't wash it?"

"Wash . . . what?"

Gifty laughed.

Auntie took the pan off the fire. "You need to wash the rice till the water runs clear. Or it will be sticky."

She went back to the living room to continue her conversation, calling over her shoulder, "Gifty, help her."

I did as she said and set the rice back on the fire. Then I busied myself washing the dishes on the draining board and tackling the large banku pot, which had been left to soak since the night before, an inner skin of corn dough detaching from its surface. I checked on the rice in between; it was coming to a boil. I was scared of burning it, but I acted cool. When I was done with the dishes, I opened the lid again. A waft of steam escaped with that boiled-rice smell. I thought of asking Gifty to check if it was ready. She had her head down, peeling ginger. There was not much water left in the pan and it would be a shame to risk burning the rice now that it smelled so good.

What if she told me the wrong thing, just to make me look stupid? I hadn't known her long, but she made me feel like I'd been wronging her all her life and owed her perpetual penance. I took the rice off the fire, drained it, and put it in a Pyrex bowl, feeling quite proud of myself.

I laid the small table in the living room. It was a simple meal—rice and mackerel stew—but I was hungry, and it smelled good. Auntie took the first bite. She stopped, mid-chew, as if she had bitten on a stone. "Abena!"

"Yes, Auntie?"

"Is this how you people eat your rice at home?"

I took a bite myself. It was slightly crunchy. And...
shoot, I'd forgotten the salt second time around.

Gifty chuckled. I felt like smacking her, but I couldn't
blame this on her.

"And you, what are you laughing at?" Auntie turned
to her. "Didn't I tell you—"

"It's my fault, Auntie," I said. "Not hers. I'll do it
better next time."

I didn't add that I'd eaten rice like this in restaurants
abroad where they called this texture "al dente." That
would definitely not help me right now. And I didn't
even like it this way myself. So I kept my mouth shut and
ignored how they were chewing as if trying not to crack
their teeth. After dinner, I did the dishes with Gifty in
silence and said good night to Auntie as she watched
GTV news with her feet up.

I could escape to my room at last. It was smaller
than my mother's walk-in closet, but it was mine. Gifty
slept on a student mattress in the living room. She had
to wait for Auntie to go to bed. At least I had a getaway.
And this precious hour or two was the only time I had
to myself every day.

I took my diary out of my suitcase, where I still kept it, and sat cross-legged on the bed. I'd never bothered much with diaries before. But now it somehow connected me with home and gave me a break from being the person they saw, the one who felt a bit ridiculous right now. My diary just made me me again.

I wrote about the day: the shop, the storm, my disastrous cooking. But most of all, about meeting Faiza. I scrolled to her photo on my phone to describe her. I wrote how we communicated without any real language. I tried to remember what I knew about her, like her town—Tolon, that was it. I wondered what it was like. I thought of what Auntie had said about the things girls carried on their heads "up there." I was still curious. But I didn't need to ask her anymore. I could ask Faiza.

Yes, that was what I was going to do.

Chapter 3

As we pulled into the car park the next morning, I wondered if we would run into Faiza again, but there was no sign of her. We'd managed to communicate that we'd find each other, but we hadn't fixed a time or place. That would have been tough not only language-wise but also because of her work and because of Auntie Lydia. I figured it couldn't be that hard, though. She knew the shop now, and I could always check the car park again later and...the one other place I knew for sure she might go to find customers—Blankson's Electricals.

I needed no excuse to go there, except to give to Auntie Lydia. Electrical shops had never been my favorite haunt, but Mr. Blankson had a pair of nephews who made his seem like the most exciting place in the world. They were brothers, Gifty had told me. Similar but different; cool as cucumbers. Also on holiday from school and working in their uncle's shop. They showed people how to use the electrical gadgets and helped with repairs of fans and TVs and stuff. And they always made sure the latest hip-hop or hiplife music was blaring from the shop.

At lunchtime, Auntie asked if I'd like some of the leftover mackerel stew from the night before. She'd brought it along in her food Thermos. Gifty would be buying kenkey on her way back from sewing class for us to eat it with. She'd be here any minute. I wasn't a big fan of kenkey and I had already eaten more of it in the past week than I ever did at home just to avoid admitting I didn't like it. But also—this might be my best chance to get out of the shop.

"Nah, I'm good," I muttered, fine-tuning my escape plan in my head.

"Did I ask you if you're good or bad?"

"Oh, sorry, I meant—no, thank you, Auntie!" I needed to pay attention when she spoke to me.

"Children of today! You can't even speak proper

English anymore. 'I'm good' indeed! Who even told you you're good?"

She started smiling and I did too. She was a crusty old thing, my aunt, but when laughter found its way through the cracks, it was ridiculously contagious. I seized the moment to ask if I could go out and choose something to eat for a change, throwing in that I'd spotted some packs of red-tinted hair at a stall yesterday. I knew she was looking for something like that for her next weave. She gave me money to get some for her on my way back.

"Don't go and buy some nyama-nyama food and get sick o!" she said as I opened the door. "I don't want your mother to say—"

"Thanks, Auntie!" I rolled my eyes behind her. "See you in a bit."

I made a beeline for Blankson's, scanning the passersby outside the shop, but I didn't see Faiza. *No need to rush off*, I thought. *Let's just go in and browse for a bit, shall we.*

One of the boys came over—the taller and lankier of the two. "Can I help you?"

Oh my, was he fine! That face deserved a designer label. "Just...looking around," I said.

"No problem; take your time. If you need me, just call."

I need you all right, I said in my head, but out loud, just—"Cool!"

I turned to watch him walk away, and that was when I spotted Faiza. She was standing outside, clasping her head pan and peering inside. I gave her a little wave and she smiled. Then she looked beyond me, and I saw a customer in the shop signal to her. The woman was just leaving the counter, loaded with bags. I hurried outside and beckoned Faiza in, nudging her in the opposite direction. I wasn't planning to buy anything, but nobody needed to know that.

I headed toward the TVs. I needed to look as if I were going to buy something heavy. The other Blankson boy was serving a customer, flicking through channels on a TV set. He looked like a broader version of his brother, with shorter hair. He glanced in our direction and said, "I'll be with you in a minute, please."

Faiza looked away timidly, but I caught something in her eye. I smiled and raised my eyebrows at her, and she covered her mouth with a hand that could not hide her smile.

"Let's get out of here," I whispered as the boy directed his customer to the counter. I led the way out of Blankson's, hoping not to bump into the woman who'd tried to hire Faiza. I headed for the stall where I'd spotted the hairpieces the day before. Best to get Auntie's shopping out of the way. Faiza hung back as I spoke to the vendor, and I realized how tricky it was going to be to get to know her. No one expected two girls like us to be walking together as friends or equals.

The wine-colored streaks in the coil of nylon hair were bolder than they'd looked as I'd hurried past the day before, trying to keep up with Faiza and her customer. I dithered for a moment. But, no, Auntie could more than carry this off. As we left the stall, I smelled roasted plantain and rubbed my tummy to show Faiza I was hungry. We walked in the direction of the smell, and I bought roasted plantain and roasted groundnuts, a combo I loved despite its nickname, "Kofi broke man," earned for being such a cheap meal.

There was a space behind the seller's stall where she kept her bunches of plantain. I asked if we could sit there. She looked from me to Faiza, an eyebrow raised, then pointed at a wooden crate I could use as a seat. Faiza used her head pan, flipped upside down. She brought out some hard salted coconut and boiled peanuts from a package she had in a pouch at her waist, and we shared our food.

"You like that boy, don't you?" I asked as we munched.

She looked questioningly at me.

"Blankson's," I said.

"Hah!" She chuckled.

I pulled my phone out of my pocket and showed her a photo I'd taken while pretending to read a message. It was of her crush, with the customer who'd bought the TV.

"Mbo!" She took the phone from me, smiling from ear to ear.

"I know, right?" I took it back and scrolled to a lopsided, out-of-focus shot of his brother. Faiza clapped a hand over her mouth and giggled.

"Those two . . . Aish!" I fanned my face. "They're like P-Square."

I saw a flicker of recognition, and I started singing the prelude to my favorite P-Square hit. *"O yie-eeh-eeh-eeh-eh . . ."*

"...O yie-eeh-eeh-eeh-eh," she took it up.

I cheered. She might be from a place I'd never heard of, but who didn't know the identical twin gods of Nigerian R & B? The Blankson boys had reminded me of them at first sight. I repeated the line, and she echoed it again. We were at the actual lyrics now, and to my astonishment, she sang, "Hello, how're you doing, my angel my one and only..."

We continued together, and her diction was perfect. I realized she knew the words by heart without understanding them. I was good with song lyrics too, but I'd never tried memorizing them in a language I didn't know! I felt light-headed with surprise, giddy with possibility as we sang on, smiling and swaying in sync from side to side till we got to the chorus and belted out together—

"No one be like you!"

We laughed in a way I hadn't laughed for a long time and were still laughing as we headed to Auntie's shop, leaving a bemused, smiling plantain seller behind us who must have thought we were crazy. The crazier thing, though, was that I felt like I was going back to alien territory. Or rather, to a place where I was the alien. That awkward feeling had completely evaporated while I was with Faiza.

We were within sight of the shop when a customer signaled her.

"Go on," I said. I knew she had to work, and I was late getting back myself. But it was an odd feeling, walking with someone who could be hailed by other people like a taxi.

"Tomorrow!" she said, surprising me again.

I'd said it to her yesterday. The girl was just a sponge when it came to picking up new stuff. She pointed at herself, then at the shop. She'd come and find me this time.

***

Auntie loved the hair and started planning her next weave straightaway. I wondered if I was ever going to see her real hair. I thought about getting a weave myself. Or braided extensions, like Gifty's. Or even going natural. There was no shortage of salons in Makola, and I was getting tired of straight-perming my hair. My roots looked as if they were fighting with the straight bits they ran into. I pulled off my scrunchie and pushed my fingers into them.

"Your regrowth, ehn?" said Auntie. "If you like, come with me when I go for the new weave. They can retouch for you."

Gifty nodded approval. "Ma, let them do something for her, please! This her hair...*mscheew*." She shook her head, threading her fingers through her own long braids.

"Oh, Gifty!" said Auntie, but she was smiling.

I knew they both thought I looked a mess. I'd brought my frumpiest clothes to Auntie's, my hair was neglected, I did nothing with my nails, and—the worst sin in their book—nothing to lighten my skin, which was darker than theirs. I would never have bleached it; no child of my father's—of my parents, for that matter—could ever have contemplated such a thing. But it felt surreal being the odd one out for that, especially surrounded as we were by all the skin "fading" and "clarifying" products in Makola. As for the rest, I'd never been good at keeping up with beauty stuff at the best of times, let alone while adjusting to a new place.

"If I was you, ehn, come and *see*!" Gifty said with a toss of her head that left me in no doubt what a disgrace to my background she found me. I had a sudden image of her in designer clothes and accessories, with skin several shades lighter and a glossy Brazilian weave down her back like a Nollywood star. And a feeling that, for once, our thoughts were perfectly in sync. Then, suddenly, with the momentum of extremes, the image switched to Faiza in her faded T-shirt and wrapper cloth, headscarf, and flip-flops.

And it hit me all over again: I was making friends with a kayayoo.

Chapter 4

THE FOLLOWING MORNING, BUSINESS WAS SLOW. IT HAD RAINED again, and the market was taking its time waking up. Auntie wanted her emails read to her, and then she left me in peace at the laptop while she lounged at the desk, chatting on the phone. She had set Gifty to dusting shelves and refolding fabrics, but Gifty was more focused on a telenovela she was trying to keep up with. The TV on the wall was never off; Auntie said the customers liked it, and I had, with difficulty, grown used to its constant noise. It still had a faded Blankson's Electricals sticker in one corner.

Mr. Blankson was Auntie's go-to for anything remotely technical. He had sourced the fridge, microwave, sewing machine, and laptop—all secondhand—and had been the one to convince her to get Wi-Fi in the shop, plugging her into some group deal for market vendors. He'd been here on my first day to discuss something about that. I could see Auntie didn't really understand how it all worked. She just kept saying, "Don't mind those people; as for me, I'm not paying another pesewa!" He told her at least she didn't have two nephews on vacation gobbling up all her Wi-Fi. I'd pricked up my ears. "But watch out for this one!" he said, chuckling and pointing at me. I didn't mind, because he had such a good nature about him. I didn't expect to have much chance to use the internet for myself, anyway.

But I'd noticed Gifty's reaction when the nephews were mentioned, and I asked her about them after he left. She grinned, for once without malice, and whispered, "Some fine boys o!" clearly pleased for a chance to talk about them. Though she'd seen them a few times, she didn't know their names.

I wished I could find them on social media. With Faiza. How fun would that be? But then I suddenly wondered: Had Faiza ever been on the internet? Did she even know what it was? It seemed incredible—though entirely possible—that she might not. I imagined her face, seeing it for the first time. Then I pictured Auntie's face, walking into the shop to find a kayayoo at her precious laptop.

I typed up my latest additions to my Makola article. I had written a bit about the kayayei. Now that I knew Faiza, they'd become more interesting to me, and I had a few questions for her.

Only two customers showed up before lunchtime, and I served them and saw them to the door when they left. The second time, Faiza was standing outside. I told Auntie I was hungry and wanted to go get my own lunch again.

In this way, Faiza and I started seeing each other almost every day. By walking me back to the shop, she'd find her next customers, and Auntie got used to seeing her around. Faiza was learning Twi and English faster than I'd ever thought possible—pidgin English through her work, and the correct version through me. I was even picking up some Dagbanli in the process. But we mainly used Twi, and as soon as we had enough language between us, I finally asked what she and the other kayayei carried where they came from.

We were in the car park, sitting facing each other on the low wall with feet up and arms around our knees. I was glad I was wearing my ripped jeans, because they made it easier to perch this way. I hadn't even packed them when I first came to Auntie's. But things were getting more relaxed, and I'd brought them from home at the weekend. Chocolate, too. I took out a bar and broke it in segments to share with Faiza.

It was one of the warmest days of the rainy season so far, and the few shrubs in the car park were bursting with new leaves, one dotted all over with tiny white flowers. It was so good to smell something other than exhaust fumes in this place.

"Water," said Faiza, munching on chocolate. "We carry water."

"Water?" I hadn't thought of that. "From where?"

"From the stream," she said logically, "to our homes." She rummaged in her waist pouch and produced a tangerine, the color of her headscarf. "Sometimes we walk the whole morning. With bowls on our heads, like this one."

"Full of water?" How could anyone carry that? And for hours. I asked how to say "water" in Dagbanli.

"Kom." She started peeling the tangerine, piling the orange skin in a neat heap on the wall between us.

"Kom," I echoed, reaching for a piece of peel and absently squirting its essence onto my hand. She stared.

"Smells nice," I said.

She took a piece and tried it too. "Mmm!" She pulled the segments of tangerine apart and handed me half of them, then put one into her mouth. "But we carry other things too, like . . . dari." She paused for a moment, chewing. "Tree . . . for fire."

"Tree for . . . Oh, you mean firewood?"

"Yes! Fire . . . wood."

"From where?" I echoed my earlier question, splitting off a tangerine segment. It was as sweet as they could only be at this time of year.

"From the trees!" She laughed. "Abba, is that not where it grows?"

She had such a cheeky streak. But you'd never know it if you only saw her as a kayayoo.

She spat out a seed. "We cut it from the trees and carry it home."

I put chocolate and tangerine together in my mouth. She watched as if I were crazy, but I convinced her to try it too.

"Mbo!" she said. "Amazing!"

"So, what d'you use the firewood for?"

"For cooking. Abba! What else?"

Her eyes danced, and her smile stretched the tribal marks on her cheeks ever so slightly.

I looked closer. "Did it hurt? When they did that to you?" I pointed to her marks and touched my own face.

She laughed at me again. "How would I know?" She cradled an imaginary baby to show how little she'd been when they were made.

My own grandpa had tiny marks too, at the edges of his eyes and lips. I'd heard Dad say it was because his mother had lost several babies before he was born; the marks were to protect him from being taken from her too. I asked Faiza what her marks were for, and she shrugged.

"Our people have them, especially the older ones. Just to show who we are."

We jumped as a car horn blared close to us, then

another, in tuneless chorus. A man leaned out of his car window. "Ah, what are you doing?"

"I'm coming out, can't you see?" yelled another man.

"And you? Are you blind?"

They traded insults and drove off. We waved away the dust from their angry wheels.

Sometimes Faiza got tired of all my questions and turned them on me. She pointed at my bare knees now and asked about the huge holes in my jeans. "Did they get torn?"

"No, I need them like this so I can sit on walls with you!"

It was my ears next. Why did I have three earrings in each instead of one? "What for?" she asked.

That was an odd question. "I dunno." I shrugged. "They're just...cool, I guess."

"Did it hurt?" She put her hands up to her ears.

"The first two, no, because..." It was my turn to cradle the imaginary baby. She nodded. "But the others? Oh yeah!"

"So...why?"

"Why did I do them?" I recalled Mom asking the same question. "Everyone has piercings, Faiza. Especially at school. You should see them. This is nothing!"

We were back to her favorite topic, school—the thing she was most curious about. She'd had no idea there was an American School in Ghana and didn't understand what I was doing there. I explained it was not only for Americans. "Dad wanted me to go to a boarding school like Holy Child or Wesley Girls' or Achimota." I could see she'd never heard of those. "But Mom said I was her only child and I wasn't going to live in any boarding house. She's the one who chose the American School."

"It must be a very beautiful school."

"That's what Mom said when we went there. I think it was the facilities that impressed her." I shrugged. "It's okay, I guess. We have air-conditioned classrooms, computerized blackboards, a big swimming pool...." I had to stop there because I feared Faiza was going to choke from all the gasping she was doing.

"Sssssss!" A loud hiss distracted her. A woman buying yams from a seller in the car park wanted a kayayoo.

Faiza's head pan was leaning against the wall between us. I wished for a second I could make it invisible so people would leave her alone. But I knew that was selfish of me. She had to earn her living, and I couldn't imagine what that must be like.

"It's okay if you have to go," I said.

But she waved her palm at the woman to show she was not free. "So... what's it like?" She turned back to me. "Going to such a school?"

"Oh God, I hate school!"

Words failed her for the first time. Then, "What happened to you there?"

"Oh, it's not like anything terrible happened. It's just, you know, school is... school. We all hate it! I mean, everyone hates school, don't they?"

She carried on staring as if I'd just told her someone had died.

"Okay, look, I didn't mean I hate it like I hate... okro or something. It's just such a drag having to go every day. Lessons can be so boring, and homework is the worst."

"You hate okro?" She looked even sadder.

What was wrong with hating okro? Didn't everyone?

"I farm it," she said. "Okro is my best crop."

It was my turn to be at a loss for words. I'd never had such a conversation in my life. What girl farmed

51

okro, for God's sake? Eating it was bad enough. What was I even doing here, sitting in Makola Market with this Best Okro Farmer kayayoo girl?

"You should see our okro back home. Not like the small-small ones in this market. They're huge and beautiful!"

I read my own horror in her eyes.

She changed tack. "And the flowers!"

Okro had flowers?

"They're so pretty. All yellow and fluffy, with purple in the middle. Even the leaves are beautiful."

I felt bad now, but I just couldn't do this...okro love. "It's so...slimy," I said feebly.

"You've never eaten the dried one?" Her eyes were wide.

Who dried okro? Why? How bad could this get?

"It's good!" she said, reading my face again. "Dried okro soup with TZ and dried fish, woi! It's my favorite."

It sounded perfectly revolting to me, but there was something about the way she said it, about the way she said many things, that made me wonder if I was the one missing something, if there was actually a lot more out there than I had a clue about. And there was something about her, about the way she didn't care if I thought farming okro and eating all that stuff no one had ever heard of was weird.

Gifty would have stopped talking or changed her story. But Faiza made me feel like I was the weirdo for not knowing those things. And laughed at me for it. And made me laugh too. And it was fun. How on earth did she do all that? "What's TZ?"

"You don't know TZ? Tuo zaafi?" It was as if I'd asked what water was. "We eat it every day!"

"Is it like fufu? You know fufu, right?"

"Of course." She laughed. "We eat fufu every day during the yam season. And when the yam is finished, we eat TZ. That one is made from corn."

"Like banku?"

"A bit, but not fermented like banku."

It was amazing to think she ate something every day that I'd never even heard of. I felt like I was talking to someone from a different country. TZ! Dried okro! Who knew?

And okro wasn't the only thing she farmed. She helped her family grow corn, millet, yams, groundnuts, beans. And she carried huge loads of foodstuffs from the farm to the house. Shea nuts too. But those weren't farmed. They were picked from trees that grew wild in the savanna. That one was tough to understand. "Kpihi," she kept repeating, making round shapes with her fingers. "Kpihi!"

I was clueless.

"Come, I'll show you."

Faiza grabbed me by the hand, and we hopped down from the wall. She led me to the section of the market where shea butter was sold.

"Okay!" I nodded at last. My grandmother used it for her skin. Auntie Lydia had sent Gifty to buy her some just yesterday. Faiza asked if I'd ever used it myself.

"No!" I said, wrinkling my nose. I didn't like the smell of it.

She laughed at me. "In my village, we eat it!"

I felt disgusted again, but then I remembered Julie Clark at the PTA school fair last semester, watching me eat wele—"Eew, gross! What is that?"

"The skin of the cow," supplied her faithful acolyte, Janice Mensah.

"*Eeeew!* You're eating *cowhide?*"

She was so annoying. There I was, enjoying my waakye rice with beef, and she was backing away like the wele was going to attack her. I felt like chasing her down the sports field with it.

I didn't want to act like Julie now. But I didn't even know why I cared. If I'd been with my mates at school, we could have laughed it off quite comfortably.

"Come," Faiza said again, and this time she led me to a part of the market where women were cooking all sorts of things.

"Wow!" I said, "it's like an open-air restaurant! I had no idea all this was here!"

We headed over to a row of women in colorful veils. They were sitting behind wooden tables, some tending huge, round pots of sizzling oil that reminded me of the kelewele seller at Labone Junction, near my house. I smelled something new and followed my nose, pulling Faiza along. I looked at the crooked brown circles that had just been lifted out of a bubbling pot and wondered what could smell this good.

"This is kuli-kuli," said Faiza.

It was made of groundnuts, she said, miming the

rolling of the paste and twisting her imaginary strip into a ring. I pulled out a coin from my pocket and was surprised how many I got in exchange. We started crunching, and from the first bite, I knew I'd found a favorite haunt. Faiza also pulled out a coin from a knot in her wrapper cloth and went over to a different food seller, squatting on her haunches and greeting her respectfully. She came back with two small blocks of something I'd never seen before. It looked a bit like soft soap, but it smelled good, and I was still hungry.

We sat on a wooden bench by the vendor's stall.

"Try it." She handed me one.

I bit off a chunk and licked a light oiliness off my lips. "Mmm!" I loved it on the spot without the faintest idea what it could be. "It's almost as good as kelewele!"

"Nothing's as good as kelewele!" Faiza's face lit up.

"You should taste the one near my house. I've no idea how they season the plantain, but oh my God!"

I thought of taking Faiza home, introducing her to new things too. The idea was exciting, but it felt odd imagining her outside this market. I wondered if she felt the same. This was the only world we'd shared so far, but it was such a small part of our lives. Just a short while ago we might as well have been on different planets in separate solar systems. I wondered who she was in hers—what made her tick, what made her smile the way she was doing now.

"D'you have kelewele back home?" I asked.

She shook her head. "Our place is too dry for plantain. I've been doing odd jobs for one of the kelewele sellers here, just to get some to eat!"

"But seriously, this stuff tastes amazing. What is it?"

"Tubaani. A sort of bean cake, steamed..." She trailed off, watching me gobble.

I'd never have guessed it was made from beans. I finished it off and glanced purposefully at the seller.

"...with shea butter!" Faiza concluded.

I stared. "You're joking."

She was laughing at me, all right, but I could see she was serious.

That was something we were always able to tell with each other, right from the beginning.

Chapter 5

I TOLD AUNTIE LYDIA ABOUT THE TUBAANI WHEN I GOT BACK TO the shop, but she cut off me off with, "Hausa food! So, now you're eating with that Hausa girl. Didn't I tell you..."

"*The broni and the kayayoo,*" Gifty taunted to the hum of the sewing machine. She just didn't understand what I saw in Faiza and wasn't even trying to hide it anymore. She was from a village too, but in the South, and to her that made all the difference. She called Faiza a "bush northerner." I knew she was genuinely puzzled that I should prefer Faiza's company to hers, especially when we were kind of family.

I tried to tell Auntie that Faiza was not a Hausa but a

Dagomba, not that I knew what the problem would be if she were a Hausa girl. But as always seemed to happen when I talked about Faiza, I couldn't seem to hold Auntie's attention beyond one sentence. She bustled over the cloth racks as if the topic were too trivial to sustain anybody's interest. She clearly didn't mind Faiza outside the shop as long as she carried for our customers, and if that meant I started eating with her, she wasn't going to forbid it outright, but she wasn't going to jump for joy over it either.

I became bolder about spending my lunch breaks with Faiza. Every time I got back, I'd be smiling at the customers and chatting with Auntie till she asked if someone was paying me per word, one of the many affectionate reprimands with which she simultaneously loved and disapproved of my ways. I knew that her own children, when they were young, would not have chatted on and on to her as if she'd been one of their mates. They never went to an expensive school full of bronis, but to strict Ghanaian boarding schools, where children were terrified of pupils a year older, let alone adults.

Auntie tolerated a lot in me with her unique brand of grumpy affection. She let Faiza hang around outside the shop, chatting to me in between customers. Our shop became her station, and she no longer roamed the market for customers. She also carried for Auntie Omotola's customers from the gele shop next door.

When business was slow, Faiza would turn her head pan upside down as a seat while I perched on the step outside the shop, the chilled air seeping deliciously into my back from underneath the door. We'd chatter away against the bustle of the marketplace in Twi peppered with English, pidgin, Dagbanli, and sign language. If we spotted a customer heading our way, we'd break off quickly, and I'd lead them in while she melted like a chameleon into the background, waiting to be called if she was needed.

I often accompanied her to the car park when she was serving our customers. Auntie had given up protesting. Sometimes we'd stop once out of sight, and I'd make Faiza transfer the bowl to my head. It just didn't seem fair, somehow, that she should always carry it. She was such a tiny girl and so skinny. I often forgot how small she was, because when she talked, and when her face split into that huge smile that was almost too big for it, she just seemed the same size as anyone else.

It was when I saw the bowl on her head, ridiculously dwarfing her, that it struck me how little she was. But she let me do it because she saw how proud I was when I was able to balance and carry it more than a few paces, and she didn't want to spoil my fun. It was more to humor me than to help her, because I struggled under it far more than she ever did.

That was why she was the kayayoo, I guess. As she explained to me, "kaya" meant "load" or "goods" in Hausa. And as I already knew, "yoo" meant "girl" or "woman" in Ga. I did not wonder at this odd mongrel of a word until much later. I just marveled over how such a tiny girl could carry such heavy loads. There was something so strong about her smallness. I envied it, although it did not seem to make sense for a girl like me to envy anything about a girl like her.

June flowed into July, and the rains reached their peak. For two days, they barely stopped. Makola became a ghost town compared with its usual chaos. One section of the market was flooded, and dozens of vendors had lost wares. The flooding was no surprise given the overcrowding in the market and the state of its drains. Nor was it any different from what happened every year, but that did not improve Auntie Lydia's mood.

Thinking up ways to escape it made me remember my plan to ask Auntie Omotola next door for lessons in gele-folding. Faiza was not around that morning, and Auntie wanted my help digitizing her accounts, but she needed to do some updating first, so I asked if I could go next door until she was ready.

Business was slow at Auntie Omotola's too, and her face lit up when I entered the store.

"Welcom, welcom, Abéna!" she said, re-inflecting my name in her singsong accent. I loved to hear her talk, best of all when she spoke Nigerian pidgin. I'd learned to tell the difference between Ghanaian and Nigerian pidgin English from the music and movies all over the market. My favorite of her expressions was "Na wa o!" which she said right on cue with the warmest of sympathy when I told her how fed up Auntie Lydia was with the weather.

She sent her assistant out for meat pie and chocolate milk for us. Then she took two geles out of their cellophane wrappers—one bright yellow, and the other, green with silver flecks. She held them out for me to choose. "I make one for you, and you make one for me!"

I chose the green.

"Good! Now, just do what I do. Ready?"

She flattened out the stiff yellow fabric on the counter. I did the same beside her with the green. Then she opened a drawer, took out a box of tiny pins, and pulled a couple of old newspapers from a sheaf in there. She lined part of her gele with the newspaper and folded it inside to create a rim. "This is how we stiffen it," she said, "like a hat."

I'd never imagined there were old newspapers inside those magnificent headpieces, but I just followed her lead, tucking mine firmly into the glossy green folds. She placed the incipient yellow crown on my head to measure it, and I measured the green on hers. Then she gathered half of her fabric into pleats around the rim and poked in the tiny pins. They disappeared completely, holding everything in place. She flared out a pleated crest behind them.

"Woi!" I said. "I mean, *wow!*"

It was like beauty origami, and she made it look so

easy. But she was a good teacher; so patient and encouraging, and she said I was a natural. When we were done, we took a selfie together in our geles. My yellow one made me think of the sun with rays flaring around it.

The meat pie was crumbly and hot, and the chocolate milk was so creamy. I felt like a VIP as Auntie Omo and I sat eating and sipping with our geles on. I wished I could spend the rest of the day with her, but Gifty's knock came before I finished my pie. I wrapped up the other half and thanked Auntie Omo, reluctantly removing my gele.

"Stop!" She held up a hand like a traffic cop. "Take it with you. And this one too." She removed hers. "Practice with them. Na your homework be that!"

"But..."

"Don't worry." She winked. "I'll get cloth from your auntie!"

Faiza was still missing in action, and Auntie's mood was no better. The shop was noisier than ever because Gifty was practicing on the sewing machine while rapping along to a Sarkodie video on the TV. She'd turned up the volume so she could hear it over the hum of the machine. Auntie didn't seem to notice. She was hunched over her old ledger, elbow on the desk, chin in hand. My glorious gele didn't seem to bring out the sun for her either. She just grunted as I came in, and went back to penning figures like she was trying to punish both the pen and the yellowing pages. Her horn-rimmed reading glasses made her look like the sternest of schoolmistresses.

I went to deposit my new treasures at the back. Gifty stopped rapping and jerking when she saw me. "Wow! You made these? They're fine o!"

"I made this one." I perched the green gele on her head, and it tipped forward with its own weight, almost covering her eyes.

"Foolish girl!" She giggled, taking it off and handing it back to me.

"How is she?" I whispered, pointing back at Auntie.

"Same!" She rolled her eyes. I rolled mine too.

I left the geles on the table and went back to Auntie at the desk. I opened a spreadsheet on the computer to copy her figures into. I wasn't even going to suggest teaching her Excel.

The laptop was as testy as Auntie. It kept freezing,

but I called its bluff each time and forced myself to wait. Restarting it took forever; it was such a glitchy old thing—like her. I grinned at the thought. I soldiered on a while longer but gave in finally, closed all the windows, shut the system down, and pressed the on button. It hummed importantly back to life, but rebooting was going to be another matter.

I wondered what Faiza was doing. I wished I could spend more of this time with her, but it was harder to find places to perch outside with this endless rain and everything drenched and muddy. And there was less chance than ever to sneak her into the shop, because Auntie and Gifty stayed in all day. Gifty's madam had canceled classes for the week because of flooding at her home. I'd asked Faiza if we could hang out at her place for once, but she'd just changed the subject as she always did when I raised it. I knew she stayed somewhere in the market, but she'd never say exactly where. I got that she was uncomfortable for me to see it, but I really didn't care what it looked like.

Maybe it was time to pluck up my courage and just ask Auntie if I could bring Faiza inside the shop. She might not mind as much as I thought. I knew she wasn't in the best of moods because sales were so slow, but that was what made this the perfect time to do it. I took a deep breath.

"Auntie, please, when we finish, can I bring Faiza inside?" There, I'd said it. I couldn't quite believe it.

"To do what? D'you see any customers in here?" She picked up the ruler and penned a red line across her columns.

"No, I mean..."

The hum of the sewing machine ceased abruptly. Auntie's eyebrows began to furrow. But it might have just been the figures. She was running her finger down a column as if something was not quite adding up. I took another breath.

"Auntie, please; you see... Faiza's my age but she's never been to school. She's so smart, but she's never even touched a computer. I was just thinking, maybe..."

Auntie's finger stopped, mid-descent, and she looked at me over the tops of her semicircular lenses.

"Abena, tell me something: Have you ever seen even Gifty touch this machine?"

"Well, no, but—"

"And you want to bring a *kayayoo* to use it?" She

67

whipped the words out almost faster than I could follow. "For her to carry it away in that head pan of hers?"

Gifty guffawed from the back of the shop.

Fury made my eyes prickle, but Auntie and Gifty would only ridicule me if I exploded, so I said quietly, "Auntie, I beg you, don't talk about Faiza like that."

"Ei! But you too, why? She's just some Hausa girl doing kayayoo in the market."

I sighed. "Auntie, I told you before.... To begin with, she's not even a Hausa, not that—"

"And so? What difference does it make?"

"Well, how would you feel if someone called you something totally different from what you are? Like... a Hausa woman?"

The sewing machine stopped again.

Auntie took a deep breath and exhaled slowly, as if to hold herself in check. She took off her glasses and laid them on the desk. Then she held up a finger at me.

"You this Abena! If not for your mother, ehn... hmm! Even my own children can never talk to me like this!" She assumed an injured air. "But as for you, just because your parents are rich, you think you can disrespect me!"

"Auntie, I didn't—"

"It's okay! I can see that all you care about is that kayayoo. A girl like you! Living in a beautiful house, going to white people's school! What would your parents say?"

She made me feel as though I should be ashamed of myself. She had insulted Hausas, kayayei, Faiza, Gifty, possibly even me; yet somehow she still managed to be the injured party. I hated to feel like I'd hurt or disrespected her, but deep down I knew I had no reason to feel that way. I also knew that I was in Ghana, in the shop of my mother's elder sister, and that, as a child, there was nothing I could say right now, other than sorry, that would be deemed respectful.

The laptop finally booted as the hostile-territory feeling began to overwhelm me. I stared into the freshly opened window on the screen. I wasn't going to apologize, but if I said another word, I'd burst into tears with the sheer unfairness of it. All the bucket baths, the cockroaches, even the possible rats, were nothing compared with this. Auntie's tirade rang in my ears, especially her question at the end. I wouldn't have minded so much if she'd left my parents out of it.

Should I be ashamed, I asked myself. Whether I liked it or not, it was certainly odd for a girl like me to be striking up a friendship with a kayayoo in Makola Market. Was it really a friendship, though? Half of me nodded—yes, of course—and the other shook my head quickly—no, of course not.

It was weird feeling like two people at once, but I knew where the no part came from—it was that growing sinking feeling that there was no world for us beyond this market. Now it was official: I couldn't even bring Faiza into the shop. I might be able to take her to my own house, but with or without Auntie Lydia, she'd never fit into my world, nor I in hers. I knew it, and it made me even sadder. How could I call someone a friend whom I could only relate to in one place? "Acquaintance" seemed more apt when I thought of ever discussing Faiza with my parents or schoolmates.

But in my heart I knew it was a friendship, had known it from that first smile we exchanged. And not just any friendship either. Faiza seemed to know what I was thinking before I said it. We hardly needed language to communicate. I loved her sarcasm, the way she could make a question seem idiotic with a simple

"Abba!" But the laughter was always for both of us; and how much of it there was! I'd never known there was so much freedom in laughter till I met her. It welled up like millions of tiny bubbles, filling us with lightness till we felt we could float away, fly in the sky, free as the birds.

Now, more than ever, I longed for it—the laughter, the freedom, the friendship.

"Auntie, please, I'll finish this later." I walked to the door without looking back.

I stepped outside, feeling like an escaped convict. I didn't care if it was still raining. Fire could come down from the sky if it liked. I was going to find Faiza.

She was right outside, leaning against the wall of the shop. The rain had stopped, but she was holding her upturned bowl as a shield against the dripping roof. *Drip-plop-tap*, went the water on the metal. She was in a reverie till I walked right up to her.

"Abena!" She smiled. Then she frowned. "What's the matter?"

"Them, inside." I pointed to the door.

She placed her bowl, still upside down, next to the wet step outside the door, took a handkerchief out of her waist pouch, and wiped the bowl dry. She patted it. "Sit! We can both fit."

We balanced ourselves on her bowl, and I braced one foot against the step. "You know, Faiza, I envy you."

"You envy me?"

"Yes! You just run your own life without anyone telling you what to do!"

"Ah, you think you're the only one with an auntie, don't you?"

"You have an auntie too?"

I immediately felt silly for asking such a question. Any moment she was going to say "Abba!" and turn to me with dancing eyes. But she didn't, and when I looked up, she said simply, "You want to know my story?"

I nodded.

Chapter 6

"I come from a small village close to Tolon," Faiza began. "I wasn't born there, but when I was four years old, my parents gave me to my auntie, my father's sister, who lives there."

"They *gave* you to her?" I interrupted. "What for?"

"For life," Faiza said simply. "That is our tradition."

"For all children?"

"Mostly us—the girls."

I guessed it must be something like Koshie being sent to us, and Gifty being sent to Auntie Lydia. But I wanted her to continue her story, so I kept quiet.

"My auntie had her own children, and I helped her

look after the little ones. And with everything else—cooking, cleaning, washing, trading, farming...When her children went to school I stayed behind, doing all that work. Sometimes when they came back from school, they would sing *A, B, C, D, E, F, G* and they would count 'One, two, three...' And I learned some of it and wanted to learn more, but I knew Auntie would never send me to school. My cousin Asana was my best friend in that house, and sometimes she would open her exercise books and show me what they had learned in school.

"One day Asana came looking for me in tears because her parents had just told her not to go back to school. They wanted to marry her to a rich man. He was one of her father's friends, except that he was older than her father. I knew that man; his mouth was full of gaps, and the teeth that were left were brown from chewing kola nuts. He already had three wives. He was quick-tempered, but everyone admired him because he owned the village corn mill and a tractor. It was the only one in the village. When Asana protested, her father asked if she was mad. She did not know what to fear more, her father's anger or marrying Alhaji Brown Teeth."

"Alhaji Brown Teeth!" I giggled. "Trust you, Faiza!"

"That was what we called him, Asana and I. She got a headache every time we talked about him, and she said the idea of getting close to him made her stomach hurt as well."

"Poor thing," I said, heartsick for this cousin of my friend, whom I had never met. "How awful to be forced to marry Alhaji Brown Teeth."

"Well, and that was not the only problem."

"How d'you mean?"

"You see, there was this boy she liked already, Malik."

"Ah! And what was he like?

"Oh, he was so cute! He had dimples, and he was always joking around. All the girls liked him in the school."

"But she was the one he liked, right?"

"You know it! You see, my cousin was so pretty, and she giggled a lot, just like you, actually!"

"Like me?" I felt like I was learning something new about myself.

"Yes, you!" Faiza said with one of her oversize smiles. "And him. They just understood each other."

"Excellent!" I said, enjoying the story and then remembering it was a sad one. "So, what happened?"

"Well, she'd hoped that once she finished school, Malik might ask for her hand in marriage, but now all her dreams were shattered. Malik was still in school, still surrounded by girls who liked him, and she was faced with becoming the fourth wife of Alhaji Brown Teeth. She cried day and night, but it did nothing to soften her father's heart. She was not the first young woman in the household that he had married off."

"What about her mother?"

"In our village, a woman cannot tell a man what to do. Auntie told Asana to stop crying and be strong, that she was not a child anymore. Auntie knew that they would get a rich dowry and that her husband had been praying for Alhaji's eye to fall on Asana, but I knew it was her daughter's misery that had tightened the corners of her mouth.

"Asana was a twin; that was why she had not been given to her father's sister as a child. Her older sisters had already gone to aunties before I came to live there. But twins are a special blessing to our people, and they don't separate them. They get to be raised by their own parents. Asana stayed with Auntie Fati, so they were close. Her twin sister had died when they were little. Sometimes she used to tell me I was like her sister come back to her.

"As soon as Alhaji made the first ceremonial presentation of kola nuts to her parents, Asana became like a prisoner. The adults in the household hardly allowed her out of their sight. They were impatient for Brown Teeth to come and take her away so that they wouldn't have to worry about anything happening to jeopardize the marriage. She felt so hurt and abandoned; she'd just sit in the room staring at the wall. Then she'd lie on her mat as if she was asleep, but she wasn't. She had cried all the tears she had, so she was just lying quietly, trying to wish herself away from there."

"So, when did the wedding take place?"

"*Abba!*" Faiza smiled and then said carefully and mischievously in English, "Exercise patience!"

I had to smile too. It was so funny but at the same time so perfectly correct, so typical of her. She picked up the story.

"Brown Teeth had traveled to Mecca for the hajj and wanted the marriage to take place as soon as he got back. That was the reason he wanted to take a new wife, to celebrate his return and his officially becoming an alhaji—the first in the village. Auntie tried to cheer Asana up by telling her he would bring back beautiful things for her from Saudi Arabia, but that only made Asana clutch her stomach and turn away. She told me she felt like a cow being fattened for the feast.

"The wedding was to take place a day after Brown Teeth's return. The imam would bless him as an alhaji and perform the marriage rites, so there would be a double celebration. The day he returned, the whole village was astir. When I got home from the stream that evening, Auntie wasn't home. She'd gone to her sister's house to borrow some jewelry for the festivities the next day. Her finest cloth—the indigo-and-white one I loved, with glinting gold threads woven into the pattern—was hanging on the line outside to air. On the line outside Uncle's room on the other side of the compound were three batakari. He would wear all of them tomorrow, with the smallest, sleeveless one on the inside and the largest, longest one on the outside, to make him look big and important. This magnificent garment—his biggest batakari—was handwoven in stripes of white and blue, with yellow embroidery on the front and back. The matching trousers hung next to it. I'd never seen him wear it before.

"The whole compound was busy. All the women of the household were cooking, because even after the bride was gone, visitors would come to congratulate her proud parents. Uncle's second wife and two other women were pounding dried corn for TZ in the mortar outside Auntie's room. They were singing along to the rhythm of their alternating pestle beats, making up a song about the wedding and laughing at each other's contributions—some rather rude.

"Uncle's sister was busy over the outside hearth, making soup in an enormous black pot and shaking her head at their song with a smile on her face. She called me over impatiently and helped me down with my heavy head pan. 'What took you so long?' She used an empty tin to slosh water from my pan into her bucket.

"As I went inside, I wondered how Asana must be feeling, hearing all the preparations and the song of the maize pounders. I found her holding a knife and staring at the sharp edge as if in a trance. She didn't even hear me till I was right in front of her.

" 'What are you doing?' I asked in fright.

"She jumped, startled. 'Chɛli ma, Faiza! Leave me alone.' She put both hands over her face, and for the first time in days, tears ran down her cheeks again. 'There is no other way out for me.' Her voice was all cracked.

" 'Di niŋla la! Stop it!' I grabbed the knife from her and returned it to the basket in which Auntie kept her cooking utensils. 'How can you even think of such a thing?'

" 'If you were me, you'd think about it too.' I held her and she cried and cried, and I cried too.

"Then I stopped and said, 'It's not the only way out, Asana. There is another way!'

" 'To run away? Faiza, if that were possible, I'd have done it already. But you know how many people are out there, and how they've been watching me.'

" 'But I'll help you!' " I lowered my voice to a whisper. " 'At the stream today, I heard a group of girls talking. They're planning to run away and become kayayei in Accra!'

80

" 'What?'

" 'That's why I was late getting back!'

"Asana's eyes grew huge.

" 'Seems they've been planning it for a while. They leave at dawn tomorrow, to catch the early bus down south! They're hoping that with all the excitement about your wedding, it'll be a while before people realize they're gone.'

" 'Leaving at dawn?' It seemed to be the only thing she had heard.

" 'They wouldn't even have told me,' " I whispered, " 'but Rakiya is part of the group, and she couldn't keep a secret from me, so they made me swear not to tell.'

" 'Your friend Rakiya's leaving? But she's no older than you!'

" 'Some of them are even younger! You know how everybody wants to go these days. Rakiya's been dreaming of it ever since she saw what the returnees brought when they came back for the groundnut harvest. She's been going on about English bowls ever since!' "

I had to interrupt Faiza's story now. Returnees? English bowls? I had to know what she was talking about.

The sun was out now, and the dripping around us had stopped. The step was dry. I rose from my cramped perch on Faiza's bowl and took up my usual post.

"Okay," she said patiently, "let me explain a few things. I'm not the only kayayoo from my village. Every year, many of the young girls leave for the markets of Kumasi and Accra."

"Why?"

"Well, they feel they'll have a better life that way. Most are with their aunties, so they know they'll never go to school. And even those in school...You know these village schools—or I guess you don't—but anyway, those schools cannot help them be anything in the future. So some of them convince their families to let them go so they can earn some money, and others just run away without telling anyone. Some come back for the groundnut harvest every year, to see their families, make a bit of money back at home, and show everyone the fancy things they've bought in the city."

"Like English bowls? What on earth are those?"

"You know those cooking pots with bright colors and designs?"

"The ones that come in stacks of different sizes?"

"Exactly! Those are what we call English bowls."

"Oh! So, what do the girls want them for?"

Faiza smiled at my puzzlement. "Where I come from, women have to collect cooking pots and utensils and serving bowls and plates in preparation for marriage."

"Marriage? You said some of those girls were younger than you!"

"We marry young in the village, and they like to start preparing early so they'll have a good collection when the time comes. They keep adding to them after marriage."

A woman walked by with a tray full of oranges on her head. We waved her over, and she came and lowered the tray by the step. We bought two oranges, and she took out her knife, shaved the peel off in neat swirls that left the pith intact, and then sliced the tops off to make them into an easy snack. We helped her lift the tray back onto her head, and she disappeared into the market.

"So, what do the girls need so many pots and pans for?" I asked, sucking juice from my orange. It was so sweet that I wished I'd bought more.

"Well, in your home, when your mother cooks, it's probably only for five or six people, right?"

My mother never did the cooking, but I knew that wasn't the point. "Even fewer." I spat orange seeds into my hand.

"In my village, a woman may have to cook for up to fifty people at a time. When it's her turn, she cooks for the entire household, and with all the different wives and their children and the other relatives, that comes to a lot of people."

"No wonder your auntie needs a helper! So, does she have a lot of bowls?"

"I wish you could see them! So many sets, all neatly stacked on a table, some as high as the ceiling!"

I tried to visualize walking into someone's room and seeing, in pride of place, of all things, a towering display of flowery pots and pans. I realized I actually wanted to see them, actually wanted to go to Faiza's home and see all the things she was telling me about. I pictured Auntie Lydia's reaction on hearing I wanted to go up north. "It sounds like your auntie's very proud of her collection," I said.

Faiza smiled, spitting seeds out too. "Back home, that is a woman's pride. They all try and get the best collections. That's why the young girls struggle to work and buy them."

"Have you started your own collection?" I asked slyly.

"Not yet, but when I'm able to save enough money, I will."

I aimed an orange seed at the road beyond the shop.

She laughed. "Are you trying to plant a tree?"

"You plant your okro; I'll plant orange!"

We threw seeds in turn, trying to see who could throw farthest.

"So, are you looking forward to getting married?"

"Oh no! Not yet, but getting my pots and pans is just something I have to do."

I understood what she meant. It was like getting something everyone else in your class had or passing an important exam. Just one of those things you had to do, whether it made sense or not.

"Faiza," I asked, "other than getting married, what d'you want to do in the future?"

"If I could go to school..." She smiled. "So many things! I don't even know which to pick first. But without school..." Her smile faded, and I felt my stomach sink as if it were my own future tied down by the lack of that one thing.

"I can teach you to read!" I said, wondering why I hadn't thought of it before.

"Mbo!" Her face lit up again. "For real?"

"Sure. That'll be a start, at least."

She jumped to her feet and grabbed both my hands, almost pulling me up. "Oh, Abena, thank you! Thank you, thank you, thank you!"

"It's okay." I smiled. "No biggie."

She stayed on her feet as if struck by some bolt of energy. "Let's get started! Now-now!"

"Now-now-now?"

She seemed to nod a dozen times in one second. There was no saying no to that face. "Sure," I said, smiling. "Just finish your story first."

She clapped her hands and skipped for a few steps before settling back on her bowl. I almost regretted my words. She'd probably zoom through the rest of the story now. She took a breath to resume and then stopped.

"Wait! You haven't told me what you want to be in the future."

"Yeah..." I stared into the market. "I'm not really sure yet. But I hope something to do with writing. Maybe journalism."

"That would be perfect for you!"

"Really? Why?"

"The way you're always noticing things around you, taking photos, asking questions..."

"*Me* asking questions! What about you?" We laughed.

"But you'll get married too, won't you?"

I shrugged. "Sure, I guess. But I'm in no hurry. There's so much else to do!"

"That's exactly how I feel! There's no way I can imagine getting married right now, especially after what Asana went through."

"Oh yes—Asana!" I was impatient to get back to the story. "So, what happened next?"

At that moment I realized that an important-looking customer was standing before us with her hands on her hips. I usually saw them before they got that close and made sure we cleared the doorway, but this time I'd been so engrossed in Faiza's story that I hadn't spotted her.

Flustered, we both jumped out of her way.

Chapter 7

"SORRY, MADAM!" I SAID WITH AN INGRATIATING SMILE AS THE customer marched into the shop. I scuttled after her with a quick backward nod at Faiza, who was already melting into her surroundings. I was nervous the woman would complain to Auntie Lydia. She looked the type, and it could hardly be a worse time for that. But it seemed my apology had done the trick, because she said nothing and allowed herself to be fussed over by Auntie, pointing at the most expensive lace fabrics. I had a feeling Faiza would be needed for this purchase.

Auntie had hit the jackpot with the first customer of the day. She was like a wilting flower soaking up rain.

It was hard to believe she was the same person I'd left in the shop.

The lady chose my favorite cloth, a peach lace encrusted with specks of diamanté that were hardly visible until light fell on them. When Auntie opened it out, a hundred tiny gems caught the fluorescent lights overhead, and I couldn't help gasping. The lady looked at me with a smile.

"You have good taste, like me!" she said with a wink. Suddenly I recognized her. She was the one who had come into the shop in the mesmerizing outfit the day I'd met Faiza.

I liked her after the compliment and was glad she was the one to buy my favorite cloth. It was the only one of its kind in the shop, and I was sorry to see it go, but at the same time I felt Auntie's pride in a good sale.

I thought of Faiza's description of her auntie's cloth with the glints of gold. I knew how she felt about it. One day, I too would own gorgeous fabrics. But I wondered sadly if she ever would. Not if she remained a kayayoo, that was for sure.

The lady also bought some high-heeled gold shoes

and a matching bag. "My daughter is having her engagement," she announced proudly.

Well, Auntie pulled out all the stops after that.

"Ayeforɔ maame—mother of the bride!" she cried,
as if announcing a star on a stage. "We have to make
you look like a queen so that when they come to take
your daughter, they will know where she is coming
from!"

The lady beamed. I could just picture her in the
peach lace and gold accessories, splendid as the sunset.
She chose two other lace fabrics, two kente cloths, and
a glittering piece of aso oke. The bride would have to
change her outfit several times, she said.

"Call your friend!" Auntie finally said to me. There
was no trace of anger or the recollection of it in her
voice.

It was almost an hour later. The woman had fallen
in love with the shop and, while chattering with Auntie,
had decided to buy pretty things for all her daughters,
not just the bride. I smiled as I stepped outside. This auntie of mine—people didn't notice when she was wooing
their money out of their pockets. She'd even managed to
get herself invited to the engagement ceremony!

I shaded my eyes against the blinding outdoors, and Faiza appeared as magically as she had disappeared. I saw a look of recognition and then of slight puzzlement on the lady's face as Faiza entered the shop and she realized that this kayayoo really was my friend. This time Auntie herself wanted to accompany the customer to the car park, so I stayed in the shop.

I pictured the engagement ceremony with all the women in their finery, looking good, smelling good, feeling good. The bride's family would sit on one side and the groom's on the other. In a stylish procession, the young women of his family would carry in head pan after head pan, balancing them perfectly on their heads like Faiza, but these ones would be made of shining brass and laden with lavishly wrapped gifts for the bride and her family.

The family's ɔkyeame, or spokesperson, would say that their son had seen a lovely flower in the garden of their prospective in-laws and had come to ask if he could pick it. She would joke and sing, and everyone would join in and be in the best of moods. After a number of items had been presented, the bride would make her first appearance, amid a procession of women shouting, "Ayeforɔ! Dondoo-o!"

In my mind's eye she was a lovely young girl draped in glittering lace and beautiful beads, smiling shyly in the middle of the noisy procession and scanning the crowd for her beloved. But then my daydream switched tracks and she turned into Asana, sad and weeping at being given to old Alhaji Brown Teeth. What different things marriage could be!

The increased volume of the TV interrupted my thoughts. Gifty had turned it up, taking advantage of Auntie's absence to pull up a chair for her favorite Mexican telenovela. A handsome man and a beautiful woman were saying how much they loved each other. Their faces moved closer as if pulled by invisible strings between their unblinking eyes. As their lips touched, I thought of Alhaji Brown Teeth again. I shuddered and turned away.

"Ah! What is wrong with you? You don't like kissing or what?" asked Gifty in the tone of one who did it all the time. That was typical of her. I couldn't help rising to the bait.

"And you? Who have you kissed?"

"My boyfrien," she said with a gesture like a rap art-ist, dropping the d in a bid to sound American. It was so annoying when she did that. She seemed to think she was impressing me and clearly couldn't see she was doing the opposite.

What boyfriend? I wanted to ask, but I thought better of it. She'd only make up some story to waste my time. I pitied her for needing to be some invented person with an invented accent and invented lifestyle to impress me. I wondered when Faiza would be back. Gifty's fakeness always made me long for Faiza's company the way I'd long for a piece of koobi, my favorite salted fish, after eating too many sweets.

As if hearing my thoughts, Faiza knocked lightly on the door. I knew it was her because that was how she knocked when she knew Auntie Lydia wasn't there, and wanted to find out if I was free.

"Your auntie said I should tell you she's going to take the lady to her seamstress," Faiza informed us. "She said you should watch the shop for her."

This was good news. With the traffic and the chat-ter those two had struck up, she'd be away for a good while. If she asked us to watch the shop, it meant she wasn't hurrying back. I was dying to hear the rest of Faiza's story, but at the same time, this was too good an opportunity to miss. There was no way to describe the internet to her without her actually seeing it for herself.

I knew how Auntie Lydia felt, but I also knew that deep down she kind of liked Faiza, if only she'd let herself past her own silly notions. I wasn't too worried about Gifty because, much as she resented Faiza, she wouldn't want to get into my bad books by reporting me. And there were all the times I'd covered for her when she wanted to go roaming in the market. I wouldn't say anything, but she didn't know that. Faiza had a right to see the internet. Everyone did.

I beckoned her inside.

Faiza hesitated, but I took her hand and pulled her in. We had time.

"Hang on," she said. "My bowl!" She went back out and leaned it against the rear wall of the shop, out of sight.

Faiza knew about computers but had never been this close to one, and she gave a little jump backward when it hummed to life at the touch of my finger. Gifty cackled, but we both ignored her. That was something Gifty disliked about Faiza—that her contempt just seemed to bounce off the girl and come right back at her. She returned to her telenovela, raising the volume higher still. I was actually glad because it gave us some privacy.

Faiza watched the changing display on the laptop screen as it booted to life, and I could almost see her thoughts racing in time. I did a search for "Tolon" and found a website that gave some facts about the area. I read them, translating into Twi where necessary.

"Woi!" she cried. "It's true! Those are the things we farm. How do they know?"

I showed her a savanna landscape photo with termite hills and shea nut trees.

"Ah! This is really our place!"

I clicked on a photo of a mosque, and as it loaded in full screen, her smile seemed to encircle her entire face. "My uncle rides there on his bicycle every Friday, for prayers!"

She was shifting from one foot to the other, pointing at the screen, putting her hand up to her mouth, then pointing back.

I told her the population of the town, and she said, "You've never been there, but you are telling me how many people live there!" She shook her head in wonder.

I read out a list of villages in the vicinity, and she laughed at my pronunciation till tears flowed down her cheeks. I laughed too, clowning around. The moment she recognized a name, she'd call out the correct version. My repeat attempts cracked us both up, especially when I tried to imitate a sound she made in the back of her throat—like a hiccup in reverse—that just didn't exist in any language I knew.

Gifty shushed us but we ignored her, and she turned back to the TV, sounding a loud *mscheew* between her teeth.

I wanted to google something else, but Faiza made me continue with the list of villages, hoping to hear her own. As it turned out, she wasn't really from Tolon. It was just the closest town to her village; something too hard to explain when we had first met. She cheered when she finally made it out through my mangled pronunciation. It was one of the real tongue twisters, but I made an extra effort, since it was her very own village, and she set herself to teaching me how to say it right.

"One day I'll come and visit you there!"

"Mbo! I will be so happy!" Then she stopped smiling. "If only you'll be comfortable at our place."

I knew what she meant, and I'd never felt like braving the discomforts of village life before, but I felt differently now.

From her village we went to America, and I showed her the Statue of Liberty. She couldn't believe people could go up into its crown. "How can something built by human beings be so big?"

So I took her to Egypt to show her what humans had built thousands of years ago. She couldn't believe they had built the pyramids just to house dead kings.

Then we traveled millions of years back to see the dinosaurs. She jumped backward again when Tyrannosaurus rex reared up on the screen.

"Woi! Nya o nyina!" She clutched at me.

"What?"

"Look at its *teeth*!"

She had difficulty getting her mind around such vast time periods and understanding that, although dinosaurs were long gone, they had lived on earth far, far longer than the human race. Even just that they had existed was a lot to swallow, and when I explained that their remains had helped create the oil we now used for petrol, she scanned my face sharply. If she hadn't trusted me, she'd have doubted her eyes and ears.

She asked what had happened to the dinosaurs, and I told her what I'd heard on a nature program: that they'd been killed by an asteroid crashing into the planet. How to explain this was another challenge, and I googled websites about the solar system and showed her the planets and tried to explain how they revolved around the sun. She asked how we could possibly be revolving around something that rose and fell in the sky every day. I said I didn't really know and she'd just have to trust me on that one.

I had never appreciated the wonder of knowledge the way I did that day, when I rediscovered the world through the eyes of someone who had never known how much of it was out there. I'd thought we'd spend the rest of our time googling film stars and fashion pages, watching music videos on YouTube, and drooling over handsome pop stars. I wouldn't have believed the fun we could have just taking in the fascination of the world around us.

"If the people in my village knew all this," Faiza whispered, "they would never believe it!"

Chapter 8

I BROUGHT MORE CHOCOLATE, SWEETS, AND POTATO CHIPS WITH me from home the following weekend. Mom had left behind enough supplies to open a shop, and they were coming in handy brokering a fraught peace with Gifty, especially in buying her silence for Faiza's visits to the shop. Gifty had a sweet tooth, and imported brands made her feel cool. I'd been able to bring Faiza in twice now—the second time when Auntie had gone to the bank.

This time I saw my chance when Auntie decided it was time to redo her weave. Gifty's madam had recommended a new salon, and Auntie was going to try it out.

"Abena, come, let's go. They can retouch your hair for you."

"Just like that? Don't I need an appointment?"

"You and your broni nonsense!" she scoffed. "This is Makola!"

We left Gifty in charge of the shop. Faiza was standing outside. Auntie gave her a nod, walking briskly ahead. I greeted her a little stiffly and then turned around and pulled a face that made her laugh and gave a secret signal to show I'd be right back.

We headed past Auntie Omo's shop, left the textile section behind, and passed a series of stalls spilling mattresses, pillows, and rolls of foam onto the pavement. Then we walked by a line of sidewalk vendors with mats on the floor selling shoes, bags, and belts piled next to pans full of makeup and costume jewelry. I'd have liked to take photos, but Auntie walked surprisingly fast for her girth and the heeled slippers in which she was clacking along, expertly navigating the open drains and treacherous terrain of Makola. We turned off sharply down a row of stalls lined with cosmetics and hair accessories. I'd not been down here before.

"Redeemer something-something," she muttered. "That's what she said. Abena, can you see anything like that?"

We passed a couple of brightly painted hairdressing kiosks. "There! 'My Redeemer Lives Hair and Beauty Parlor'" I read over a doorway.

It was a large wooden kiosk painted in turquoise and pink, every inch on the inside covered in posters of hair-dressed women and dangling sachets of nylon hair claiming to be Brazilian, Russian, Indian. The counter was crowded with hair tongs, different-sized combs, racks of acrylic nails, and flamboyant nail varnish bottles. A glass-fronted cabinet held brightly labeled pots, jars, and bottles of every imaginable substance for the styling of hair and the lightening of skin.

Dryer hoods hummed over two women in rollers, one of whom was also having her nails done. A third was having her hair braided in a spiral around her head, ready for the nylon pieces to be sewn on, and a fourth had three girls in orbit, plaiting her hair into endless braids.

A woman came forward.

"Auntie Connie?" asked Auntie Lydia.

"Yes, madam!" She smiled and pressed an elaborately manicured hand to her chest. "Welcome!"

She too had a face lighter than the rest of her, even lighter than Auntie's, and she reminded me of Auntie in her manner. I wondered how the two would get along, but Auntie Lydia smiled and said, "I left my old hairdresser to come here o! I hear you are great!"

A smile rippled Auntie Connie's face like water into which a pebble had been dropped. Auntie Lydia took her sachet of wine-colored hair out of her handbag, and Auntie Connie examined it. They chatted for a while about what she wanted, and Auntie Connie called a girl to attend to her. Auntie Lydia nudged me forward and asked about my retouch. Auntie Connie exclaimed what a pretty, well-spoken niece I was, but all the same, I'd have to wait till one of her other girls was free.

"Auntie, please, can I go back and wait in the shop? I'll come back in half an hour."

She agreed, eager to get started with her hair, and I ran back.

Faiza was standing outside. I pulled her into the shop with me and woke the laptop impatiently from electronic sleep. I clicked on YouTube, and we watched a couple of the latest pop videos, singing and dancing along while Gifty sewed furiously behind the screen, making as much noise as she possibly could. She'd positioned herself so she could see us, and she was spinning that handwheel fit to pull a muscle.

Faiza asked if I could show her the sun and the planets again. She was still trying to figure out the things I'd told her.

"*Abba!*" I said. "Seriously?"

She laughed. Science, entertainment—it was all discovery to her. I tried to imagine what it must be like to find out about the solar system at this age. I'd be excited too.

But our trip into space was interrupted by a customer. As the door opened, I pushed Faiza away from the computer, and she grabbed a broom and busied herself with it at the far end of the shop. The customer wanted some costume jewelry, and I brought out several sets from the standing glass cabinet. She chose one, paid for it, and left. As I put the others away, I lingered a little, arrested by the way in which the light brought them to life, like sparkling rainbows. Faiza put down her broom and came over to look too.

On an impulse, I put one of the necklaces around her neck and pushed her in front of the mirror.

"*Woi!*" She was horrified and delighted at the same time. She made to take it off, but I stopped her.

"Don't worry. Auntie's far away. Let's have some fun!"

I hooked the matching bracelet onto her wrist and slipped the dangling earrings into her ears. We both looked into the mirror and laughed. The flashy jewels were so incongruous against her faded T-shirt and wrapper cloth. I grabbed a glossy piece of sea-green sateen from the fabric rack, passed it under her armpits, and tied it at the back, ignoring her protests. I went behind the screen to grab a box of pins from the sewing table. Gifty tried to smack my hand, but I skipped out of her way, back to Faiza, and tucked and pleated the material here and there as if I were Auntie Omo. It fell to her feet and flowed out around her.

I took a wine-colored, sequined lace from the display cabinet and cinched it around her waist like a wrapper cloth over the green sateen. I draped a matching piece around her shoulders to hide her T-shirt completely. While she pleaded with me to stop the madness,

I went to the cupboard and took out the gele I'd been practicing with since my lesson with Auntie Omo. It had become quite a hobby. I was particularly proud of my latest arrangement, with its rows of folds tied into a knot at one side and opening out into a coquettish sideways fan on the other.

I tried to remove Faiza's small headscarf.

"Woi!" she said again, holding on to it.

"What's the problem?"

"We Muslims don't just remove our head cover like that o!"

"I'm so sorry!" I'd forgotten in my excitement. "But we'll cover it up again. Look!" I showed her my majestic headpiece.

"Mbo!" In a flash she had whipped off her small scarf and stashed it in her waist pouch.

I crowned her with the green-and-silver gele.

We looked in the mirror again, and this time nobody laughed. Faiza looked like a different person. I saw things in her I'd never seen before. The angles of her head-dress accentuated her high cheekbones. The rich fabrics against her skin brought out its velvety smoothness, and the kohl she always wore stood out sharply against the whites of her eyes, which sparkled as if competing with the jewels hanging from her ears. The tribal marks on her cheeks now lent her an exotic look, like a queen of an ancient empire.

"Faiza!" I breathed.

She smiled her immense smile, making this new portrait of herself even more spectacular. Gifty appeared behind us in the mirror, staring at Faiza as if she had never seen her before. It was as if a magic spell had frozen us all in time. Then Gifty broke it, coming back to her usual self with—"You two are really looking for trouble now."

I opened the door and peeked outside, but there was no sign of Auntie or of any customers heading our way. Still on a high, I told Gifty to mind her own business and gave her some money to go and buy sweets for all of us. It would get her out of the way for a bit and make her less troublesome. She'd already finished the ones I'd brought from home and had been pestering me to buy more for her.

After she left, I took down one of the ready-made boubous and slipped it over my head. It was purple with elaborate embroidery all the way down the front, from neck to hem, in pink edged with gold. I put on another set of costume jewelry with glittering pink stones. I ran a comb through my hair and fluffed it out, tying the matching purple strip around it. I shot over to the small bathroom at the rear of the shop, grabbed a pink lipstick from the toiletry bag Auntie kept on the sink, and streaked it across my lips. I took it with me and did the same to Faiza.

We stood next to each other in front of the mirror, like women who would need to be presented with many head pans full of luxurious goods before anyone could ask for the hand of their daughter in marriage. We each folded our arms and stood back-to-back, our profiles against the mirror. For once, Faiza matched my height because of her headdress.

"Who do you think I am?" I asked in a queenly voice, with an extravagant gesture of my hand. "How dare you bring these nyama-nyama things to ask for my daughter's hand?"

Faiza spluttered.

"Sister, what do you say to this presumptuous young

man?" I continued, turning toward her with my nose in the air.

"Never!" She recovered from her laughing fit and slipped into her role as if she'd rehearsed it. "Can you not see that we are queens? Look at our robes and our jewels. We shall never give you our princess." She gave a disdainful flick of her hand. "She is too good for you!"

We laughed so hard that we didn't hear Gifty come back in.

"Auntie's here!" she hissed, out of breath.

She'd tried to stay ahead of Auntie Lydia, but I spotted her through the gap in the door, just a couple of paces away.

Faiza and I looked at each other with our hearts in our mouths. Disaster was upon us, and there was nothing we could do about it. But just as Auntie Lydia put her hand on the door handle, Auntie Omotola called out from next door.

"Mama Lydia, this your hair na fire!"

"You like it?" Auntie's hand rested on the door handle.

"You fine o!"

"Thank you, my sister!"

The door handle moved down. We braced ourselves.

"Mama Lydia, I hear your new best friend is a minister's wife, abi?" Auntie Omo wasn't done yet. News traveled fast in the market. So, that was who that lady was, I thought, still rooted to the spot. No wonder.

"No be small o, my sister!" Auntie lapsed into pidgin too. They both spoke English well enough, but Auntie always preferred speaking Twi with her friends, and as Auntie Omo spoke no Twi and Auntie Lydia no Yoruba, they chose pidgin as a more convivial vehicle of communication.

Auntie Lydia's hand remained on the door handle, pushing it slightly ajar while she spoke to Auntie Omotola. If she had just looked through the crack, she'd have seen us standing frozen inside, like dolled-up statues. As she lingered at the doorway, I felt a rivulet of sweat slide down the nape of my neck to the hollow of my back, yet my fingers and toes were cold. I realized I was trembling. With a superhuman effort, I steadied myself and started to formulate a plan. Here was a chance—albeit slim—to avert disaster, and it would be foolish to miss it by succumbing to panic.

I motioned to Faiza, and we both backed slowly and noiselessly out of Auntie's line of sight. If I prayed hard enough...Yes! She was releasing the door handle and turning away, toward Auntie Omo's shop. I knew my auntie; she couldn't resist showing off her new conquest. She was going to have a little gossip before she came inside. Of course, Auntie Omo would be hoping to benefit from this hot new customer. After all, she was right next door, and as she'd told me during our lesson, every good lace needed a good gele.

There was no time to lose. I grabbed Faiza's hand and pulled her out the door, risking everything on the chance that Auntie would keep her back turned. A fleeting glance through Auntie Omo's open door showed her leaning over the counter, gesticulating with her hands to add more flavor to her florid account of the day in pidgin.

The risk had paid off; we dared not linger. I pulled Faiza in the opposite direction, rounded the first corner, and dashed into an alley, where the hubbub of noise and activity drowned out our panic.

We leaned against a wall, panting for breath. I looked at Faiza.

"Na wa o!" she said, and we burst into hysterical giggles. It felt like we would never be able to stop laughing, but a man in a nearby shop called out to us, "Happy sisters, come and look at my things!" We looked at him and then at each other. "I have lovely things for beautiful ladies like you!" he continued, pronouncing it "byuriful" in an attempt at an American accent.

A fresh round of giggles broke out but gave way, finally, to sobriety as the reality of our situation struck us with full force. In our flight and relief at escaping, we had forgotten what we looked like. Now we realized what we were being taken for—real rich ladies.

I will never forget Faiza at that moment. She turned toward him with perfect poise, her fanned headdress profiling beautifully, and said in English more polished than I had ever realized she possessed, "Why not?" And she pulled me by the hand toward the shop.

I felt as if I were walking with a stranger, and the sense of unreality grew as we browsed through the fancy goods, acting for all the world as if this were what we did every day. Faiza made it so easy. She would hold out a dress on a hanger and say to me, "How about this one?"

And I would hold it against myself, hemming and hawing while she cocked her head to one side and made comments in flawless English like, "No, not your color, not your style!"

How did she do it? And then I remembered how she'd sung in English at our first meeting. Of course, she'd been watching her customers, the rich ladies who shopped at boutiques. She'd had plenty of opportunity to study the ways of a madam. And she'd have supplemented this by memorizing phrases she heard in films. The market was such a vast and public space, and it was easy for a kayayoo to catch snatches of videos and telenovelas. But now she actually understood the words.

What made her performance so amazing was that it wasn't just the language she mimicked so perfectly; it was the mannerisms too. Gifty would have been green with envy. But that was the difference between them. Faiza only did it for a laugh. She would never be anything but herself with people who mattered to her.

The shop attendant's face mirrored the rise and fall of his hopes as we played out the scene, holding in our laughter till we'd extricated ourselves and rounded another corner.

"I can't believe he took us seriously!" My sides ached with laughter, and I could hardly get the words out. Faiza was doubled over, one hand steadying her gele as she shook with mirth.

When I look back, I can't believe we were laughing and fooling around instead of getting out of those clothes as quickly as possible and finding a way to return them, and ourselves, safely to Auntie's shop. But we were girls drunk with adventure, taking courage from each other, and we couldn't resist venturing into more shops, doing our rich-ladies act. The more seriously we were taken, the bolder we grew.

I can't remember who pulled whom, but somehow we both knew where we'd end up. And, sure enough, there we suddenly were in front of Blankson's Electricals. We'd always managed to pass it on our way to the open-air restaurant and almost everywhere else we went together, whether or not it was really on the way. We still didn't know the names of the gorgeous ones, so we'd just nicknamed them Peter and Paul after the P-Square twins.

They'd seen us before but had never really noticed us until now. We were younger than them, and they had customers aplenty and probably no shortage of pretty young things making eyes at them.

But today was different.

"May I help you?" asked our Peter.

He was almost as cute as his brother, and well built too—you could see that despite his long-sleeved shirt. He looked at Faiza, a half smile playing on his lips, and the confidence she'd displayed in the other shops wilted under his gaze.

I came to her rescue. "We want to buy a TV, please," I heard myself announce.

He led us to the TV section, not taking his eyes off her. There were dozens of television sets, and they all seemed to be showing different things, including, on one, an episode of Mr. Bean. Faiza started watching it.

The other brother—our Paul—came up. "Hey, Stephen..."

"I'm serving a customer," Stephen said quickly.

"Ah, right!" He flashed a crooked grin, white against black, that was lent a roguish air by his mustache. He was more casual than his brother, in a T-shirt and jeans, but he had a fresh, spicy scent about him that made me inhale so deeply I felt light-headed.

I looked over at Faiza to see what she thought of him, but she was absorbed in *Mr. Bean* and had started chuckling in spite of herself. Stephen was laughing too, and then they'd look at each other and laugh harder. It reminded me of how Dad always said he and I had our funny bone in the same spot.

I realized "Paul" was talking to me, wanting to know what type of television set we wanted. Oh dear, I hadn't thought of that.

"Plasma!" I said, with sudden inspiration.

"Plasma!" He seemed impressed, and I gave myself a silent thumbs-up. But then he said, "Sure, come this way."

Shoot, they had them. We walked away from the other two, and he showed me a number of plasma screens, but I found it much easier to take in the details of his appearance than the specs of those TV sets. Still, I pretended to be fascinated, because that way I could keep him talking and flashing that grin that gave me a pleasantly wobbly feeling in my stomach each time.

"No one be like you," I sang in my head.

"So, which one is it going to be?" he asked finally, jerking me out of my daydream and to the inconvenient reality that I must now buy a TV.

"Oh, um...well, actually, I'm not sure they're compatible, you see."

"With what?"

"Our whole—you know—*system* back home." I threw in a self-evident shrug.

"How d'you mean?" he studied my face and I hoped there was no lipstick on my teeth or anything stupid like that.

"You know...analog, digital, that sort of thing," I bluffed.

"What?"

Oh dear, I was in trouble now. "Okay, maybe I'm not explaining it very well. It's just that—Dad told me to make sure it was compatible, and to tell the truth..." I pulled a helpless face. "I'm really not sure what he meant!"

It worked. The ice was broken.

"Well, dada bee"—he flashed The Grin—"you'd better tell Dad to come himself!"

I grinned too. "Thanks, P—I mean, er..."

"Mike," he supplied, holding out his hand.

I shook it. He asked for my name and said it was a pleasure to meet me.

I felt the same way.

Chapter 9

As we headed back to the shop, I had more to worry about than Auntie Lydia wringing the magic out of that unbelievable day. It was almost dusk, and whatever I told her, it was going to have to be good.

"We need a place to get changed," I panted, walking at double speed.

"I know a couple of quiet corners." Faiza kept up with extra-long strides. "I use them for prayers. Speaking of which, I'm late for my evening ones."

"How about your place?"

She looked uncomfortable.

"Oh, come on! How come you never want to take me there?"

"I've told you, it's not really a 'place.'"

"Come on, Faiza! We've been through this before."

She stopped and turned to me. "Okay, the truth is, Abena, I don't have a place to stay, only a place to sleep."

"Isn't that the same thing?"

She sighed. "You see, this is why I didn't—"

"Look, just explain it to me, okay? Please."

She smiled like a mother at a toddler. "Come with me."

We headed in the direction of Auntie's shop but turned off down a row of stalls with cosmetics and hair accessories. I recognized it with an uneasy feeling; it was the way to Auntie's new salon. I was able to take in the surroundings better this time, and I turned my head from side to side, staring at wigs on plastic manne-quin heads—long, short, wavy, straight, black, brown, copper, platinum—and wondered what they'd look like on me and on Faiza. Maybe that could be our next adventure.

I bumped into her.

"We're here," she said.

"What?"

She'd stopped at the exact spot I'd meant to hurry

past—My Redeemer Lives Hair and Beauty Parlor. Luckily, for some reason she also seemed to want to stay out of sight, and we hovered behind long strips of fake hair dangling in packs from a stall opposite the salon. Through the doorway, I spied Auntie Connie working on a customer's nails. I could smell the chemical she was applying from where I stood.

What were we doing here? There was nothing remotely like a house, an apartment, or even a room nearby. I tried to pull Faiza past before someone saw us, but she held me back, pointing at the kiosk.

"Faiza, have you gone crazy? This is a salon! *Auntie's* salon!"

"*Woi!*"

Why did you bring me here?" I whispered urgently.

"I told you." She couldn't meet my eye. "I sleep here."

"But there's nowhere to sleep!"

"There will be." She ducked behind me suddenly.

I started to wonder if the excitement of the day had been too much for her. "Faiz, what's going on?"

"I don't want the madam to see me."

I glanced back inside the kiosk. Auntie Connie had looked up from her work and was staring straight at me.

I fought down panic, reminding myself what I looked like right now. There was no recognition in her eyes.

Faiza pulled me slowly away while keeping out of sight.

"Why are you trying to hide?" I hissed.

"If she recognizes me in these clothes, walking around with someone like you, she'll raise my rent."

"Rent?"

"We pay her."

"*We?*" I asked. Was I dreaming? If so, I needed to wake up. This was too bizarre.

"Me and the other girls. We come when she closes at night and leave in the morning, before she opens."

"You sleep in this...kiosk?"

"We kayayei have no homes here. All these salons..." She gestured around her. "They're our bedrooms at night. We spread our mats on the floor."

"Dear God! How many of you in this one?"

"Almost twenty."

I pictured her and the other kayayei, crammed likes sardines into this poky kiosk reeking of chemicals, snatching a few hours of hired sleep between each day's labor. And I'd thought I had it bad at Auntie's. I felt embarrassed for many things at once, including nagging her to bring me here.

"So, now you know."

I couldn't say what I was feeling. I wanted to help her. How, I had no idea. But I mustn't sound like I pitied her. Pity just never seemed like something she needed, not even now.

"Where d'you keep your things?" I asked finally.

"In bags, on top of the shelves."

Twenty girls! They couldn't own much more than the clothes on their backs.

Now it was her pulling at me. "Come on, Abena. We need to get these things to the shop!"

I came back to myself. We also needed to think up a good story for Auntie Lydia.

Faiza steered me to a deserted alley, where I excused her to do her evening prayers. Then we strategized as we removed our fine feathers, shook them out, and folded them as neatly as we could. Faiza tied on her small headscarf, and we ran back into the market, a pair of fourteen-year-old girls again.

When I walked into the shop, Auntie had the exact expression on her face that I'd expected. But I was ready. Before she could open her mouth, I cried, "Oh, Auntie! Your *hair*!"

She smiled, caught off guard, and put a hand up to it.

"It's a-*mazing*!"

"You like it?"

"I knew this color would look great on you! Gifty, didn't I say it?"

Gifty watched me with a smirk as she swept the floor.

"Thank you, Abena!" Auntie tried to wipe the pleasure off her face, "And now, young lady—"

But I wasn't done yet. "Oh, Auntie, you'll never believe what happened to me today!" Attack was the best defense, I'd decided.

"What?" Alarm broke out on her face. I felt a pang of guilt, but there was no chickening out now. I gave thanks she had her back to Gifty.

"This customer came in and selected some things," I began.

Auntie nodded.

"Then, when it was time to pay, she looked in her

bag and looked in her bag." I drew out the story to steady my nerves. "But she couldn't find her purse."

"*Mscheew!*" Auntie hissed through her teeth. "They should find their purses before they open the door!"

"She told me it must have dropped in her car and that she'd give me the money if I came with her to the car."

"And you did?" Auntie butted in.

"She begged me! Isn't that so, Gifty?"

Behind us, Gifty gave a noncommittal grunt.

I continued smoothly. "I didn't know what to do, Auntie! But I had a bad feeling about the whole thing, so I took Faiza with me just in case."

Behind Auntie, Gifty was shaking her head slowly. I tried to blur her out of my vision.

"The woman said her car was far away because she hadn't been able to find a parking space. We walked and walked, sweating in the sun, till we'd left the market behind. Then, when we were on a quiet street, she tried to grab the things without giving me any money."

"I knew it! She was just a thief, and you fell for it."

"Auntie, please, I'm sorry." I hung my head. "That's why I didn't return to the salon, you see. It took ages to walk back."

Auntie sighed. "She thought because you were children, she could take advantage of you."

"But Faiza didn't let her get away with it." I perked up. "She held on to the bowl, and the things fell on the ground. We raised the alarm, and the woman got scared and ran away."

"So, where are the things?"

I opened the door and beckoned Faiza in. She greeted Auntie timidly and lowered her bowl.

"They got a little dusty, but we shook them out, and here they are." I scooped out the remnants of a magical day and placed them on the counter, where they turned back into impersonal bits of shop merchandise.

If Auntie's new weave hadn't put her in such a good mood, she might have been more skeptical, but with the goods returned and everyone safely back, she had little motivation to make a fuss. A stern look from me in Gifty's direction while Auntie inspected the goods made her turn away and busy herself with packing up for the day, so her face would be safe from Auntie's scrutiny. I'd have to be nicer than ever to her now.

Chapter 10

My article about the market was almost complete. I'd stopped writing in my diary and spent my evening hours on it instead. I'd decided to submit it for an additional category within the junior journalists' competition, called Urban Bustle. Auntie allowed me to use the laptop at home, so I did the layout and added the photos.

It was coming together nicely, but I needed to fill in a few more details about the kayayei. It would help to hear the rest of Faiza's story about her cousin and the girls who'd planned to run away. I was still curious about what had happened to them. I wished I could ask Faiza to write a few things down for me. How she'd have loved to! She was so excited about the article and the competition. But we were still on the basics of reading and writing. She was picking it up fast, but we just didn't have enough time.

There'd been a run of sunny days, and the market was busy. It took a full week after our dressing-up adventure before we got to spend a lunch break together. We went to the open-air restaurant. Faiza said she felt like eating kenkey, so we bought some with freshly ground chili and fried fish. I had never liked fermented foods but I'd started to warm to banku because it was so good at Auntie Lydia's. I still found kenkey a bit strong, though.

Faiza chuckled at the look on my face as she peeled the corn husks off the steaming white ball. "Go on," she said.

The fermented smell hit me, and I wasn't sure I could do this after all. "Is TZ like kenkey?" I demurred.

"It's not fermented like kenkey," she said. "It's made from corn flour, not corn dough, like I told you last time. You know what, let's just get you some!"

"We can get it here? Why didn't you tell me before?"

"I didn't know you were ready to eat it." She grinned. "Look how you're making your face over this small kenkey!"

She covered her plate, and we headed for the women with the colorful veils—to one I hadn't been to before. Faiza selected a soup for me that was full of chopped-up green leaves she called "bra"—with a rolled r. I'd never seen or heard of it before.

We settled back on our bench. I pinched off a piece of TZ and tried it.

"Hmm." I nodded. A bit bland, but at least it wasn't sour.

"You have to eat it with the soup!"

I dipped my next piece in the soup and scooped up some leaves. It tasted of groundnuts and other rich flavors all new to me. "Mm-mm-mm! You guys eat like this every day?"

"Ours is fresher because we farm it ourselves."

"Where has this been all my life?" It was hard to think of anyone who ate such food every day—and fresh from the farm—as poor.

"You and food!" Faiza grinned. She squeezed the fiery red pepper sauce from a tiny plastic bag onto her plate, pinched off a lump of kenkey, and dipped it in. "So, where did we get to in the story?" she asked, munching.

"The night before the wedding."

"Ah yes. the night I caught Asana staring at the knife. That was when everything changed. Not only for Asana; for me too. The two of us had to hurry up and decide everything before Auntie Fati got home."

"Oh yes, she'd gone to borrow the jewelry from her sister, hadn't she?"

"Yes," said Faiza, "and she could be back any moment. Asana whispered to me, her face coming back to life, 'I want to be on that bus at dawn!'

"'You will, my sister,' I promised her. I had no idea how I was going to do it, but I was surer than I had ever been about anything else in my life——I was going to get her on that bus. We whispered together until Auntie came back, humming to herself and displaying her booty of gold and beads. She had drunk pito beer at her sister's house in early celebration, so she was jovial and a little drowsy. I'd seen Auntie drink pito before, and I knew that when she got the chance, it wasn't just one cup. I was jubilant. She'd sleep well.

"I, on the other hand, chewed kola that night. It was the bitterest thing I knew, but it kept people awake, and that was what I needed to be. Asana and I slept on mats on the floor, on the other side of a raffia screen that gave Auntie privacy in her bed. Asana lay there, unblinking, while I swirled the mash of kola around my mouth. The taste alone was enough to keep me awake.

"Auntie Fati snored for a couple of hours, but I needed her to stop. I knew her sleeping patterns, and the snoring stage was when she could easily wake up. When she stopped snoring and her mouth hung help-lessly open, saliva trickling out a corner; that was when she could sleep through a thunderstorm. At last, I heard the blessed sound of silence. I walked right up to her. I even dared to light a small stub of candle, which I placed inside an empty tin to dim the light.

"She was gone, all right. The beery scent still hov-ered above her, and I turned away, nauseated, yet feeling a tug at my heart for what she would face tomorrow. Asana was upright on her mat. It was time. I beckoned her over. I was going to need help.

"We went to the table that held Auntie's stacks of pots and pans. Auntie always tied her money inside her wrapper cloth, but her bank—which she only opened once a week—that was somewhere else, and even Asana didn't know where.

"I lifted the smallest pan from the tallest stack. Its enamel finish was a warm cream color, with fluffy-petaled flowers painted on either side in blue, red, and yellow, edged in silver. I handed it over to Asana, who spread her wrapper cloth on the floor and placed the pot gently on top, cushioning any clinking it might make. By the time she turned back to me, I was holding out the second pot. She took it and placed it next to its smaller twin, then folded the cloth over the inverted lid of the larger pot, picked up the smaller one and placed it delicately on top.

"She repeated this each time I handed her a larger pot, lifting the stack with greater care as it rose higher and higher. I, for my part, had to be extremely careful not to knock down any of the surrounding stacks on the table while I worked.

"After five pots, Asana needed me not only to help her lift the new stack without it toppling over, but also to lend my own cloth for wrapping and cushioning. Against the daily hubbub of village life, Auntie could easily unstack and restack these pots without anyone noticing, but in this still night air, the smallest clink was audible. It might not wake her, but one never knew who else might be awake or wandering around outside. And although we were only communicating with sign language, I knew that in our heads we were both hearing the cacophony that would rouse the whole village if one false move brought these stacks crashing down. Our every impulse was to rush, but we knew that a single careless slip could cost us everything. We handled Auntie's precious pots like raw eggs, working in a slow motion of soundless, nameless dread.

"At last, the tenth pot—a mammoth vessel—was exposed. I lifted its lid into the air, and there, wrapped in a headscarf at the bottom, was Auntie Fati's bank.

"If we were lucky, she wouldn't be visiting it for some days. Still holding the cymbal-like lid in my left hand, I wondered how much Asana would need to make it to Accra. Accra! Imagine that my own sister-cousin might be there the very next day if we pulled this off! I wondered what that huge city was like. The biggest I'd ever been to myself was Tolon, not even Tamale. I dared not take too many notes for fear of making the theft noticeable. After all, I wasn't going anywhere myself. I'd be there to face the music.

"The hoot of an owl nearby made us both jump, and I nearly dropped the huge lid. I looked at Asana urgently. It was no owl; it was Rakiya! She was great at that sound. It was the signal we'd agreed on. I had told her it was I who'd be coming with them, because I knew she and the others would be too alarmed by the prospect of the bride joining their fugitive group. After all, they were relying on the festivities as a smokescreen for their departure. But once they were on the point of leaving, an argument would create too much of a disturbance, so I was counting on the urgency of the moment for Asana's acceptance.

"Trembling, I set down the huge pot lid and grabbed the wad of notes. I peeled off a few, not even seeing their denominations in the dimness or having any idea if what I was taking was far too little or far too much. We were simply out of time. I thrust the small roll into Asana's hand, embraced her, and turned her toward the door. She was trembling too. She turned back to grab the little bag she'd prepared from its hiding place, then pointed anxiously at the pots. I gestured back—*Don't worry, I'll deal with them*—and pushed her through the doorway.

"Rakiya and the others were crouched in the bushes outside, signaling their haste. They couldn't even see it wasn't me. Asana turned back, and we hugged again for the last time. Then I watched her dart over to the others and, together, without losing another moment, they all ran away."

"Yesss!" I cheered, realizing I'd been holding my breath. I'd also stopped eating. I resumed now, pinching off a chunk of TZ and dipping it in the soup. It was cold, but I didn't care; it was still delicious. "So, did they get away?"

"Yes!" Faiza went back to her food too, picking bones out of her crispy fish. "They made it! At least I assume so, because that was the last time I ever saw them."

"Your cousin, your sister Asana, you haven't seen her since?"

"No." There was real sorrow in Faiza's voice. "I've looked, but I haven't found her."

"Where?"

"Here! In Accra; in this very Makola Market."

"So that's why..."

"Yes, Abena; that's why I'm here."

We chewed in silence while the market bustled around us.

"And your auntie let you go?"

Faiza nodded. "She was never the same after Asana left."

"Poor thing."

"It's been so hard for her."

"You...love your auntie, don't you?"

Faiza smiled. "Like how you love yours."

It was my turn to smile. There were not many people we could have admitted this to.

"Not that it's been easy, Abena. But sometimes I think I understand Auntie Fati better than anyone, even Asana. And I know she loves me too, in her own way."

We were done with our food. The kenkey seller's assistant, a girl younger than us, brought a jug of water and a bowl for washing hands.

"Shoot!" I'd spilled soup on my blue T-shirt. I used the water to clean it, leaving a wet patch all over my front.

"Don't worry," said Faiza. "The sun is out; it will go now-now."

I pulled out a bottle of hand sanitizer from my purse and squeezed a blob into Faiza's hands, then mine. We rubbed our hands together, and for a few seconds, the clinical scent overpowered the medley of food smells all around us.

Faiza picked up her head pan from the side of the bench and tucked it under her arm. "Zo!"

"That's 'come,' isn't it?"

"Mm-hm."

"Dagbanli?"

"Hausa."

"You know Hausa too?"

"Small-small. Everyone does! You hear it all over. You see, even you know 'zo.'"

"True!" I just hadn't known it was Hausa. Being with Faiza felt like a constant discovery of things that had been around me all along.

We started walking back to the shop, and I noticed a soup splotch on my jeans that I'd missed. "Jeez! Serves me right for being such a pig."

Faiza gave a pig grunt, and we laughed. "The way

you chopped that TZ and bra, my sister, you're ready for the North!"

The time felt right for another question I'd been wanting to ask her. "Faiza, do you ever miss your real mom? And your real dad?"

She smiled. "Not the way you mean."

"What way is that?"

She slowed her steps. "The way you say 'real' mom, 'real' dad. I don't remember much of my life with them before I came to Auntie Fati. I see them when the family gets together for funerals and things, and we're always happy to see each other. But my home is with Auntie."

I felt a little sad for her, but she didn't seem sad for herself, and that made me feel a bit silly, like it was my problem if I didn't understand other people's ways of life.

We walked past the vegetable stalls, and, as usual, the colors made me think of the flag. Tomato for red, garden egg for gold, okro for green in this patchwork nation of people who knew nothing about one another.

"Faiza," I asked, "why do people give their children to their aunties?"

"Abba, go and ask them!" she said in her cheeky way.

"But I'm asking you," I countered for once.

"I think they're afraid the children will spoil if they stay with their own parents. That's what Auntie Fati used to say when she got annoyed with Asana. 'I should have sent you to your aunt! You think you could talk to her like this?'"

"Really?"

"Don't mind her. She was just bluffing. Look at her now!"

"And her other daughters, they went to their aunties?"

"All. She was left with only Asana and the boys. Even them, two were given out. Alhassan to the uncle, and Sani to the grandfather."

"How many children did she have?"

"Eight. More, even, but some died. Our people have plenty children."

We were close to the shop now. I could see Gifty outside, cleaning the window, her back to us.

"But why split up the family?"

"You see it as splitting the family. Our elders see it as keeping it together. It all depends what family means to you. Our people feel that sharing children makes them all one family and makes them stronger. Mothers, fathers, aunties, uncles, grandmothers, grandfathers— living together, farming together; the children are for all of them. That's why we don't talk of 'real' parents. Life is hard, so people have to stick together."

"All the same, it must be tough...for the mothers and the children."

"Abena, when life is hard, you also have to be hard."

Chapter 11

FAIZA'S STORY HELPED ME COMPLETE MY ARTICLE, AND I SENT IT off at last, a day before the deadline. But the things she'd said about family lingered in my head. And those words—*When life is hard, you also have to be hard.* They made me think about Auntie and about Gifty. People saw the North and South as so separate, but in many ways, they weren't that different.

Auntie Lydia's daughter called when we got home that evening, and I wondered for the first time if Auntie missed her children. They were grown up, but they'd lived abroad for years. I knew that from Mom. I watched Auntie chatting away to her, sprawled on a chair in the living room in her faded pink kaftan with the joromi embroidery that gave her tummy that 3-D effect. They were talking about the shop and about business, but still, it was the most relaxed I ever saw Auntie.

I thought of some of the things Mom had told me about her. I'd been asking more about her each time we spoke. Mom didn't know all that much either, but still a lot more than I did. She told me how hard Auntie had worked to send her children abroad. How they'd raised the money for her to open a shop after years of cloth trading, especially Pat, the daughter she was speaking to now. She bought and shipped fabrics for Auntie. "That shop's all she has," Mom had said when I complained about Auntie's strictness. "I know she's a bit gruff and all that, but you have to understand."

Gifty and I were in the kitchen, getting dinner ready. Auntie had left a pot of garden eggs boiling on the stove. Gifty was on a low stool in the corner, grinding kpakpo shitɔr in the asanka grinding pot. I stood at the table peeling yam, slicing the skin off in quick, forward strokes, the way I'd seen the two of them do it, while quietly savoring the wafting aroma of the fresh green chili and the sound of the tapoli wooden grinder in Gifty's hand, gathering the little scotch bonnets between coarse grains of sea salt to crush them up against the ridges of the clay pot. Soon she would add fresh stem ginger, and the smell would become even more irresistible.

Auntie ended her call, came back, and removed the pot from the stove. She poured the water into the sink in a great cloud of steam, then began removing the skins from the halved garden eggs. They'd gone from crispy yellow to a mushy, mushroom color, and their puckered skins came off easily.

"I'll do it, Auntie!" I said.

I'd already set the yam to boil on the stove. She passed me the garden eggs and a little bowl of water to dip my fingers in so I didn't burn them. Then she poured bright orange palm oil into a saucepan. It was half-solid, but it slid quickly across the pan, beginning to bubble and give off its fruity aroma. She cut up onions with her quick, deft strokes and dropped them in. Gifty handed her the asanka, and she scraped the ground ginger and chili into the pan. It all sizzled together and made my mouth water. Auntie cooked with herbs and seasonings we didn't use at home, and with locally made oils like palm, groundnut, and coconut, which lent their fragrances to the food. The difference between her kitchen and the food that came out of it was like that between her house and her shop.

She handed me the empty asanka. "Abena, mash the garden eggs."

Gifty handed me the tapoli, and I mashed them easily into a pulp while she tossed fresh tomatoes and herbs into the blender. The electric din blanketed all sound for a few seconds. She poured the mix into the pan, and Auntie stirred it all together for a while.

"Abena, garden eggs." She reached out.

I handed her the asanka, and she scooped the pulp into the pan and mixed it in till the oil and tomatoes tinted it orange. I hated purple eggplant, but these yellow ones made the most delicious stew.

If you had told me a month and a half ago that there was anything I'd come to like about being in this grimy little kitchen, I wouldn't have believed it. But now I was actually enjoying being a part of this motley trio, working together in the calm of daily routine with a common, satisfying purpose. I made up a tongue twister in my head as I watched Auntie:

She stirs simmering stew in the steaming steel saucepan on the stove.

My phone rang. I went to mute it but I saw that it was Dad.

"The baby's here!" he said. "Your new brother!"

"*Oh my God!*" I put my hands—still smeared with bits of mashed garden egg—up to my cheeks. "Oh my God!"

I looked at Auntie Lydia and Gifty. I couldn't stop smiling. "My baby brother!" I said, and suddenly tears came. What was this? It had never happened to me before. Only adults cried when they were happy, and it was so weird.

Auntie Lydia was looking at me with a little smile I hadn't seen before. She turned back to the garden egg stew and sprinkled seasoning salt over it while I stopped to gulp and take deep breaths.

Gifty was clapping her hands excitedly. "Ei, Ba-by!"

"But how come Mom didn't tell me?" I asked Dad, wiping the corners of my eyes.

"He was premature," said Dad. "Delivered by C-section. It all happened very fast. Your Uncle Frank called me. They had to rush her to the hospital late last night. But he says not to worry, that she and the baby are perfectly fine. We should be hearing from her very soon. Your uncle's just sending me photos now. I'll forward them to you as soon as we're done."

Auntie Lydia sent Gifty to the container store around the corner for two Cokes and a bottle of Guinness. "We must celebrate! I'm an auntie again o! I'm an auntie again!" She jigged, pumping her hands as if she were on a dance floor.

Dad said Mom needed to recover from her operation, and the baby had to have his shots, so they wouldn't be back till the end of the holidays. And he had more news—my cousins Brit and Tiff were arriving on Friday. And coming to visit at the weekend.

"Oh!" I said.

"Just *oh*?"

It wasn't only about them. In my early days at Auntie Lydia's, I couldn't wait for my weekends at home. After the first week, I'd felt as if I were seeing my house for the first time. Chiffon curtains over French windows, silk cushions on leather sofas, Persian rugs on cream carpets, all in an air-conditioned cocoon. I couldn't believe I'd never noticed before how all the colors matched as if they'd been put together by design—which, of course, they had.

Then there was the food. Pierre, our chef, could make just about anything. I liked Ghanaian food and had come to love it even more at Auntie's, but she stuck to the same dishes most of the time. It was great to be able to eat completely different things again, like potato salad, fillet steak, cheesecake.

But it was the spotlessness of the entire house and the orderliness of life around us that struck me the hardest. Beyond our sprawling garden and wrought-iron gates, there was no loudspeaker din from charismatic churches, no car horns blaring, no call of street vendors. No yawning sewers when you stepped outside the walls and no stench of gutter water or rotting garbage. Just more mansions with tidy gardens. How could cleanliness and calmness suddenly seem like the greatest luxuries in the world?

Once I'd met Faiza, it became even more striking. When I went to my bathroom, I suddenly realized I'd never wondered what she did for a bathroom. As the shower gushed like my own personal cloudburst, I wondered how many head pans of water I was using.

Would I run it like this if I had to carry it myself? The mere thought seemed absurd, and I wanted to laugh at myself for thinking it, but somehow I couldn't.

I stopped going home on the weekends Dad worked. Dinah was off weekends, and Koshie had gone back to her family in Dad's hometown for the holidays. Going all the way to Labone just for warm showers and continental food didn't seem worth it anymore if I could hang out with Faiza instead, even if it meant sitting through the endless, deafening Sunday-morning services at Auntie's apostolic church. And Saturday was our best day at Lydia's Palace, so Faiza was around all day, hanging with me in between carrying for our customers.

"Brit and Tiff are going to be in Ghana till school reopens, right?"

"Yes, but they can't wait to see you," said Dad. "Britney says wait till you see what she's got you!"

"Okay. Sure." I sighed, holding in the *Whatever!* "I'll come."

Chapter 12

KOFI, OUR DRIVER, ARRIVED FOR ME ON SATURDAY MORNING. When I got to the house, Dinah was in the living room vacuuming the carpet, even though she was supposed to be off, because she wanted to congratulate me on my new brother and didn't want to miss the cousins. She'd known all of us since we were born. Pierre was busy in the kitchen. He still remembered their favorite dishes. Dad had promised to dash home from the clinic to join us for lunch.

I went up to my room. Its tidiness made me feel almost a stranger. It was weird, but I kind of wished for a tiny bit of mess just to welcome me back. Dinah always kept it spotless, no matter how I left it. She'd put the air conditioner on for me, so the room was cold. My Barbie dolls had been rounded up and confined to their swanky multistoried house. I stared at them for a moment, living out their glamorous little pretend lives. Maybe it was time for them to go. My books were stacked in perfect order on the shelves. I opened my night table drawer and put my diary back inside. I wasn't using it anymore, and at Auntie's there was always the risk that she or Gifty would come across it. I could do without the drama of them meeting themselves in there.

I heard the muted blare of a car horn through the closed windows. A silver Land Cruiser rolled up the driveway. I ran downstairs.

Britney flung open the front door and jumped on top of me.

"Ab-Fab!" she shrieked.

"Brit-Lit!" I grinned, realizing I'd missed her too.

Tiffany followed in less of a hurry, checking her phone en route. Their driver and our day guard brought up the rear, laden with packages and carrier bags with foreign and duty-free logos. There was so much stuff from Mom, Auntie Adjoa, and Uncle Frank. The driver handed a set to Dinah that had to go straight in the fridge: chocolates, candies, cheeses, hams, patés, smoked salmon, bottles of wine and one of brut champagne that Tiff said came with congrats from their dad. She picked out a tagged set of bags that she said Mom wanted me to take to my aunt at the market.

Brit's jeans were shredded from the thigh down to the carefully frayed hems, and she had even more ear piercings now, with studs and dangling crosses and stuff going the whole way around each lobe. None of it made her look any older.

After lunch, she sat cross-legged on my bed, and I thought her jeans were cool, but I couldn't decide whether I liked how much of her ashy knees were poking through. She kept fiddling with her new phone and talking loudly to Siri.

Tiffany lay on the carpet with her feet up on my bed, holding her phone over her face. She was messaging her boyfriend back home between giggles and loud dings. Her hair was shaved at one side with the rest long and flowing, and her cycling shorts and turquoise crop T-shirt showed off her new belly button ring.

"She did it without telling Mom!" Brit said enviously.

"Wow! What did Auntie Adjoa say?"

"*Mscheew!* What can she even say?" asked Tiff, skipping fluidly between Ghanaian and American English. "I'm seventeen now. I did it in London." She grinned. "While she was busy babysitting your baby bro."

"So . . . she hasn't seen it yet?"

"Nah, but she said I could do what I like when I turn eighteen. And seventeen and a quarter's nearly there, right?"

The studded hook skewered through her navel looked painful, but it had a rhinestone at the end with a sparkly letter N dangling from it.

"N?" I asked.

"*Duh!*" said Tiff with an eye roll.

"Nicky!" Brit whispered loudly.

"Oooh, *Nicky!*" I sighed, and Brit and I went into mock swoons.

"She'll be tattooing his name on her forehead next!" Brit giggled.

"Shut it, Brit-Nit," shot Tiff.

Britney pulled a face at her sister. "Let's just ignore her. Who needs big sisters, anyway? You're the lucky one! How d'you get to have a baby brother? And he's sooo cute! You're gonna just die over him—right, Tiff?"

"Whatever," her sister mumbled, tapping rapidly into her phone.

"Siri, show me pics of Auntie Theresa's baby!" Brit held her phone out to me.

I'd seen Uncle Frank's photos last night, but these were different, taken up closer, by Auntie Adjoa. My new brother was tiny and fragile, but I could see he looked like Mom. I was happy for her because everyone always said how much I resembled Dad.

"Ooh, that reminds me. Look what we got you!"

Brit grabbed her phone back from me and thrust a gift bag with purple and gold diamond patterns into my hands. "Open it, open it!"

It was a set of phone cases, a different one for each day of the week. They were in shades of pink, peach, purple, and gold, and all of them had liquid in which glittering hearts, stars, or flowers were floating. A couple had bows attached to their backs, and one had a pair of cat's ears set with pink diamanté. I thought they were amazing, but there was one problem.

"What d'you mean, they won't fit your phone?"

I showed her my new phone. "I got it for my birthday."

"Oh! Same as mine." She seemed put out, and I could tell it wasn't just about the cases. There was no more chatting to Siri after that. She moved on. "Guess what else! Mom and Dad said you can stay with us for the rest of the holidays!"

"Yeah, Mom mentioned it."

"How cool is that! Can you come today? Like, now? Go on, I'll help you pack your stuff!"

I wished I could feel, or at least look, more excited. Two months ago, I'd have been dancing around the room.

"Most of my stuff is at Auntie Lydia's."

"So, you can go get it, right? Tomorrow?"

"Um, let's see, I'll need to talk to Mom and Dad first."

"But Auntie Terry said it's fine!"

"I need to ask Auntie Lydia too."

"I can't believe they sent you there!" Brit rolled her eyes. "Like, how are you even surviving?"

"Yeah," chimed in Tiff, "Mom said she has a shop in *Makola*! You're not having to go *there*, are you?"

"It's not that bad, actually."

Tiff looked up from her phone. "Jeez, Abs, you're not going all *local* on us, are you?"

Where did one even begin with these two? "Look, I know it sounds weird, but there are actually some pretty cool people in Makola."

"You're joking, right?" Tiff was still looking up from her phone.

I paused. This was where I could have just said "*Duh!*" and we'd have laughed and I'd have packed my stuff and got in their car and we'd have spent the rest of the holidays going to the mall, eating pizza and burgers, watching movies, swimming in the pool at their Trasacco Valley mansion, and hanging with their kind of people. And everything would have been back to normal.

But normal wasn't normal anymore.

I took a breath. This was going to take some guts.

"Seriously," I said, "there are."

There was silence for a few seconds as they both stared at me. Then they chorused, *"Whatever!"*

I had breakfast alone with Dad the next morning. We video-called Mom and saw my new brother in real time. I loved his baby noises. Mom looked tired and couldn't move much because of the operation, but Auntie Adjoa was fussing over her, taking the phone and making sure we got to see the baby properly. There was something about the way she took charge that reminded me of Auntie Lydia. These my aunties! I felt suddenly lucky to have them. And a momentary stab of envy. Mom and Auntie Adjoa reminded me of Faiza and me. How wonderful to be sisters and best friends at the same time. It must have been something like that for Faiza and Asana.

Uncle Frank and Auntie Sarah came into the frame and said hi. Dad thanked them for taking such good care of Mom. "You must come to Ghana and let us 'retaliate!'"

Everyone laughed, and Uncle Frank pulled my cousins Kobby and Kojo to come say hi too. *"Aw, Dad, no!"*

I heard their London accents in the background, but as I knew only too well, there was no escaping family greetings. They came and said their awkward hellos. "Hey, Abs!" Their smiles came to life when they saw me. "How's Ghana?"

Mom asked to see me again. "Sure everything's okay, baby girl? All still well at your aunt's? 'Cause with your cousins there now—"

"I'm fine, Mom, don't worry."

"Well, if you're sure..."

I wished I could tell her about Faiza. I knew she'd be shocked at first, but when I explained how we were like her and Auntie Adjoa, she'd understand. But not right now, with everyone listening. Uncle Frank probably wouldn't even remember what a kayayoo was. Auntie Adjoa would be horrified. And terrified I would expose her precious Tiff and Brit to my market life.

"Totally, Mom. Honest!" I smiled my warmest so she'd believe me, because it was true, and because I needed her to save all her energy for getting better and for my baby brother.

She smiled my favorite smile, and I felt relieved. "I love you, Mom."

The picture went funny, and I realized she was hugging the phone. A wave of longing washed over me. We ended the call, and I loaded my plate with pancakes and drizzled over one of the syrups Brit and Tiff had brought. It was so yummy.

"Dad, you can deliver babies, can't you?" I asked.

"Of course!" he laughed.

"Then why couldn't Mom have stayed?"

"Doctors aren't supposed to treat their own family. You know that, Abee."

"But you have a whole clinic! Couldn't Dr. Ampiah do it? He delivered me! And there are other hospitals in Ghana."

"I know all that, sweetheart, but it was your Auntie Adjoa who talked her into going abroad."

"Auntie Adjoa thinks there's nothing good in Ghana."

Dad had that stifled smile on his face that adults got when they agreed with you but couldn't say so. "You know what you women are like. When one talks another into something, no one else stands a chance!"

I thought of me and Faiza and the things we'd put each other up to.

"To be fair to your aunt, though, your mother's on

the older side now as far as having a baby is concerned. And with the asthma...It's better to be safe than sorry, and the hospital where she had your brother is better equipped than anywhere in Ghana. We could never have afforded it at the time you were born."

I opened a small pot of jelly and added some to my pancakes. There was a whole gift basket of syrups and jellies. I made a note to take some to Faiza. But today I was going to spend the rest of the day at my cousins' house as a compromise.

"So, are they kidnapping you till Mom gets back?" asked Dad.

"Yeah, about that," I began, and then stopped, not sure how to continue. I cut another piece of pancake and chewed on it.

"I don't think Brit's going to take no for an answer." He smiled.

"I don't think Auntie Lydia is either, Dad."

He cocked his head. "What's going on, Abee? I thought you'd be thrilled to be rescued like this!"

"Auntie kind of relies on me now, to help her with the computer and stuff."

"That's very responsible of you, sweetie," he said, "and you know I was all for you having a change of scene and all that. And you've done fantastic! Even better than I expected." There was a pride in his words that sent a warmth through me. "But you should have some fun too, for what's left of the holidays."

"I am!"

"Your auntie will manage. Don't worry. I'll speak to her."

"No! Why won't you guys believe me? I *am* having fun. It's different, but different can be good, like you keep telling me, and I...even have...a friend at the market."

"Really? That's great! Someone your age?"

"Yes."

"Also spending the holidays there?"

"Well...yeah."

"Cool! What school does she go to?"

That helpless feeling came over me again. Assumptions. That was it. People didn't even know they were making them, but they stole the breath from what you wanted to say—what was already hard enough to say—and left it strangled, mute. I'd thought Dad was the one person I could tell that Faiza was a kayayoo. Now I just didn't know how to do it.

His beeper went off. "Here we go!" He finished his tea hurriedly.

"Hang on, Dad. There was something I wanted to ask you."

He set his cup back on its saucer, trying not to look as if he was in a hurry. "Shoot!"

I felt shy suddenly, but he was looking at me expectantly.

"What's a dada bee?"

He laughed. "Just another version of 'dada ba.'"

"I know, but what is that...exactly?"

"You don't know?"

"I know it means, like... 'spoiled child' or whatever, but is that all?"

"Well," he thought for a moment. "Technically—you know some children here are sent to live with their relatives, like Koshie..."

"And Gifty—Auntie Lydia's niece...kind of."

"And even me; I was partially raised by my uncle. So, the point is, a dada ba—literally 'Dad's child'—is one who is not given to relatives; in other words, is raised by their own parents."

"Like me?"

"No comment." He chuckled. "You see, in the old way of thinking, people believe children get spoiled when they're raised by their own parents, making it harder to train or, like...prepare them for life. Even today, in some places it can be a luxury to be raised by your own mother and father."

A luxury to be raised by your own parents! I'd have to get my head around that one. *When life is tough, you have to be tough.*

Dad looked at his watch. "I have to run now. Bye, my little dada ba! Have fun with the crazy cozzies!"

I waved him off. I knew he thought I'd change my mind about moving to their place. I'd had a great weekend, but I was ready to go back.

I went into the kitchen to take the bags for Auntie Lydia and some of the little pots of jelly and other goodies up to my room before I went and left them behind. The jellies were still in their gift basket with a ribbon and a tag from Harrods in London. All kinds of flavors—the usual strawberry and raspberry and all that, but crazy ones too, like onion and charcoal. They were going to blow Faiza's mind. I ran upstairs and then stopped on the landing and came down again. I went back into the kitchen and took two more pots of jelly. Strawberry and raspberry. For Gifty.

Chapter 13

I HAD FUN WITH BRIT AND TIFF THAT AFTERNOON BUT COULDN'T shake off a certain restlessness as we lazed by their pool, then watched movies in their upstairs lounge. It wasn't quite the alien-territory feeling, but to my shock it did remind me of it—without the attendant anxiety; more an unsettling sort of... apathy. I wasn't sure what was happening to me. Maybe I was losing my mind, but getting back to Auntie's felt like a relief.

She sent me to the bank for her the next morning. I told her I wanted to take photos of that side of the market on the way back for my school project. What I really did was have a late breakfast with Faiza. We sat on a low bench by a tea stall at the open-air restaurant.

We bought white bread rolls from a girl who was walking around with a large tray of them on her head. They were so fresh, they were still warm. The tea from the stall came ready-mixed with sugar and milk powder. The seller was a boy not much older than us, with reflective sunglasses and a front-to-back baseball cap. His menu was premixed tea, coffee, Milo, and bread with eggs—boiled, fried, or made into omelet. He stirred our tea into mini whirlpools that were still swirling as he set the cups before us. The brew was strong and supersweet.

"Egg?" he asked.

"No, thanks," I said. "We're good."

But we borrowed a plate and a teaspoon from him and took turns spreading jelly over our rolls. I could bet that gourmet treats from Harrods had never been eaten in such a way in such a place before. But combined with the fluffy bread and the overpowering tea, they tasted even better than at home with the pancakes. Faiza loved the jellies, just as I'd known she would.

"Mbo!" she said, munching. "Common onion! Common charcoal!"

"I know, right!"

"So, people are making charcoal into food while

we're burning it, ehn?" She had a way of rolling her vowels and consonants together that infused instant life into her words and made the humor sizzle up like smoke through coals. And she'd chuckle so infectiously between the words that I felt like I'd never stop laughing. "We use charcoal for stomach medicine in my village, but I never knew you can make your stomach happy with it like this too!"

"I didn't either," I said.

"And we have these things plenty too o!"

"What?"

"Charcoal. Onions. Most of what you see here in Makola—it's north they bring it from. When I was coming down south, I saw the trucks on the road, loaded like something. I'm telling you, if Auntie Fati hears of this, she will stop farming and become a businesswoman!"

As she walked me back to the shop, we passed a charcoal truck unloading, and she cracked me up again with, "Look at them throwing good food around like that!" Then she stopped abruptly. "Wait, I just remembered...."

"What?"

"I watched the sun setting last night."

"Ah!" I smiled. This again.

"It was moving so fast, but I was standing still."

I knew what was coming. It was a shame we hadn't yet had a proper chance to go back into space via the internet.

"Last time, you told me we are moving around the sun and—not that I don't believe you—but..." She furrowed her brow. "Are you sure you heard your teacher well? Is it not the sun, rather, that is moving?"

I sighed, starting to get an inkling of what Galileo must have felt like. What was it going to take to convince this girl? I glanced around me. "Okay, wait!"

We were just entering the fruit section of the market. Oranges were piled on the ground in great yellow pyramids. It was the peak of the season. Women in straw hats with brims wide as coffee tables were sorting through and stacking the fruit in smaller pyramids of five, eight, twelve, in their stalls. Limes lay by the hundred in head pans like Faiza's and in small enamel bowls in the stalls. After asking the women's permission, I grabbed an orange from one stall and a lime from another.

"Hold up the orange in your hand like this and stand still," I said to Faiza.

She obeyed, ignoring the ripple of exclamations from the market women.

"Right." I pointed at her orange. "This is the sun!"

"Sun." She nodded. "Wuntaŋa."

"Wuntaŋa," I repeated.

"You're improving." She smiled, trying not to move as she held her orange like a statue.

I pointed at my lime. "This is us, planet Earth—the world."

"The world." She nodded. "Dunia."

"Dunia," I echoed. That was easier. "Now watch." I moved my lime in a full circle around her orange, coming to a stop exactly where I'd started. "This is one year."

The market women looked on, some smiling, some frowning. One waved her hand to shoo us away. "Don't bring your juju here!"

"Juju?" cried the orange seller. "Ei, bring back my orange o!"

"Aunties!" I said. "Abba! This is no juju; I'm just trying to show something to my sister."

169

They wanted to know more too, so the citrus section of Makola Market became my classroom. I wasn't very good at science, but, thank God, this was one lesson I'd understood precisely because of the demonstration I was now attempting to replicate. My science teacher would have been proud of me. I made another circle around the orange for the benefit of the market women who had joined class late, as it were.

"Do you understand?" I asked.

Faiza nodded. Some of the women did too. Others didn't look so sure.

"But one thing," said Faiza. "I think you've mixed up the orange and the lime. Shouldn't the lime be the sun? It's just a small, round circle in the sky."

"No way!" I looked at the eager faces around me, feeling the power knowledge gave. "Trust me, that's just because of distance. You see, the distance between them is far more than we humans can even imagine! And because of that, the difference in size is actually far, far greater than between an orange and a lime. In fact, we shouldn't even be using an orange at all...." I broke off and looked around me. In the distance there was a building with a round plastic water tank on its roof. I pointed at it. "What we really need is something more like the size of that poly tank over there. And even then..."

There was a collective gasp. How could the sun possibly be so much bigger than Earth? That thing up there in the sky? Was I sure?

I nodded gravely. "And there's something else. I've shown you how Earth moves around the sun to complete a year. But I haven't shown you how it moves in a day."

"Let me guess!" Faiza took the lime out of my hand and circled it around the orange, making tiny stops to indicate each day.

I couldn't help smiling. She was so eager. And she never allowed her lack of education to stop her from applying her mind to figure out how things worked.

"Good try!" I said. "But Earth never stops moving; that's why we have day and night. The sun is what gives us light, you see. If Earth stood still, the countries facing the sun would always have day, and the ones on the other side would always have night."

Faiza looked enlightened and confused at the same time.

"Try again!" I said.

The market women considered the problem. I had to smile watching them try to put their heads together in their huge straw hats. They waved their arms around to demonstrate their theories and called out a wild range of suggestions. Faiza still held both orange and lime and was trying out different things, listening to them while focusing her own mind on the problem. Finally, she said, "Hold the orange for me!"

I did.

She held the lime in one hand and, while moving it around the orange, gave it a little twist all the way around, with her other hand.

"One day!" she said.

All heads turned to me. I nodded, and the market women erupted in applause. Faiza had done it for all of them. They praised her brilliance and she beamed, still spinning the green Earth on its axis while rotating it around the yellow sun, completing the full circle of a year.

Chapter 14

GIFTY GAVE A SOUR LOOK WHEN I GOT BACK TO THE SHOP. SHE knew I'd been with Faiza, plus she'd had to hold the fort because Auntie was busy in the storeroom. Gifty never liked dealing with customers alone because she was not confident about her English. She put on a fake accent but got the grammar wrong. She acted like she didn't care, but I knew she did.

I gave her the pots of jelly. I could have given them to her at home, but I was learning to time my gifts. She smiled in spite of herself, and I wondered, not for the first time, if she and I could have been friends if Faiza hadn't come into our lives. But I'd never know, because no matter how nice I was to her, she couldn't forgive me for liking Faiza. Gifty didn't know exactly what we'd been getting up to lately, but she knew we were having fun, and she resented it.

Another reason she was out of sorts was that the TV was on the blink. Missing a single episode of her tele-novelas was her definition of a crisis in life. No wonder the machine had conked out. If Auntie could see the way she ignored customers when her shows were on or made them shout above the love declarations of the Mexican soaps, the Bollywood singing of the Indian films, and the melodrama of the Ghanaian and Nigerian ones, she'd have disconnected the box herself. But now she gave in to Gifty's nagging and called Mr. Blankson.

"I'm so busy, Wɔfa," she purred into her cell phone, absently fingering the seam of her weave "I beg, can't you just send one of your boys to pick it up?"

One of your boys?

I sat bolt upright in front of the laptop where I was checking Auntie's mail for her. *Calm down*, I told myself. Mr. Blankson had several young men in his shop. It was more likely to be an apprentice in pungent overalls than Mr. Fresh n' Spicy. But that didn't stop my heart racing.

I was both wrong and right because it wasn't an

apprentice. But it was not him either. It was his brother Peter; I mean Stephen. As he stepped into the shop in a sleeveless black T-shirt and jeans, I wondered where Faiza was. I looked hurriedly away, focusing on the customer I was serving, who was taking her time finding a matching trim for a cloth she'd chosen. I couldn't afford any revealing exclamations with Auntie around. She was sitting at the corner of the sewing table behind the screen with a partial view of the shop, adding up something on her calculator.

"Abena, help him take it off the stand," she called. I was much taller than Gifty, and the TV was perched at a precarious angle. She didn't want any accidents. I felt an impossible combination of dread and delight as I asked Gifty to take over my customer. She was well peeved because she'd been checking out Stephen from the moment he'd entered the shop. No one needed to tell me he was shortly to be starring in her kissing fantasies. That would keep her going till the TV was back. She acted as if she hadn't heard me and crowded around us, pretending to make herself useful, heaven knew how.

As we lifted the TV off the stand, Stephen gave a little gasp, and the machine tipped in my direction. It was dusty and I sneezed. "Pardon me," I said, embarrassed at not being able to cover my mouth.

"Bless..." he began as I heaved the TV back toward him, "...You! You're the—"

"Shh!" I hissed. "My auntie doesn't like me talking to boys."

"I get it," he steadied the machine. "No worries."

His smile reminded me of another. Gifty looked from him to me. Behind us, the customer was bent over the trimmings, holding her blue-and-white cloth up to them.

"Just one thing, though," he whispered over the TV. "Where's your friend?"

Gifty's face froze.

"Oh, her! Um, she's around."

The door opened, and two more customers entered the shop.

"Around?" Stephen looked hopeful.

"Yeah, not too far away, actually."

"Abena, aren't you done?" called Auntie.

"Almost, Auntie!"

Stephen balanced the TV on his knee. "So...does she come to the market often?"

I shrugged. "Sure! To, like...do her shopping and stuff."

"Yeah, she looked like a classy lady." He grinned. "What's her name?"

Gifty wasn't even trying to close her mouth now. The customer was pointing at a roll of trimming, trying to get our attention. Luckily for Gifty, Auntie couldn't see her.

"Her name? Oh, it's...er..."

"Abena, why are you people taking so long over that TV?" Auntie called out. "You're disturbing the customers. Hurry up!"

I gave Stephen a *See what I mean* look, and he responded with a sympathetic *Na wa o* look.

"We're done, Momee," he piped up, wrapping the cord around the TV and walking out with it under his arm.

Gifty tried to catch his eye as she sauntered toward the customer, but he didn't notice. He gave me a wink as I closed the door behind him. It was an unfinished-business sort of wink. I didn't look back at Gifty. Instead, I asked Auntie if I could go for lunch. I told her I was hungry. I grabbed a duster to wipe the dust off my hands and was out the door before she could respond.

Faiza walked over as soon as I stepped outside.

"Did you...?"

"Yes, I saw him."

I fiddled with the duster, not sure what to ask next, but she saved me the trouble. "He walked right past me, coming in and going out."

"He didn't see you?" I gaped.

"Of course not."

"I guess, carrying the TV and all...or was he looking the other way?"

"He was looking at me, all right. But you see, Abena"—she spun her empty head pan on its edge—"looking and seeing are two different things."

"Oh!" I felt like crying, just thinking what that must have felt like for her.

"Are you trying to tear up that duster?"

"I just...got my hands dusty taking the TV down with...Oh, Faiza, it's so unfair!"

She leaned the head pan against the wall. "It's okay, Ab. You can't blame him."

How could she be this calm? I looked at her with new respect as she continued. "How can you expect him to connect the...princess he saw two weeks ago with some kayayoo standing around in the market?"

I heard an echo in my mind from our crazy make-over day—*We'll never give you our princess; she's too good for you.* I didn't know why I was remembering it. It seemed so inappropriate right now. I looked at Faiza. She might not look like a princess in her green headscarf, faded T-shirt and wrapper cloth, but, gele or scarf, it was the same elfin face beneath—so alive, so alert—the same that had laughed with him over the antics of Mr. Bean. How could he miss that?

It was those pesky things again. Assumptions.

"He was asking about you," I said miserably. "Inside the shop."

"Was he?" She let down her guard for a moment. "So, then, he recognized you!"

"Yes."

She didn't seem bitter, and her silent resignation made it all fall into place. Of course he could recognize me—the middle-class girl who might have been back from a wedding with her buddy and browsing the boutiques before going to her auntie's shop. But how could the gorgeous girl at my side possibly be an illiterate kayayoo from a village he could not have pronounced in a place he would never go? I felt all the remaining glow of that magical day evaporate like dew in the merciless sun. "He recognized me when we were taking down the TV."

How different this was from how I'd imagined telling it to her. And yet, what had I expected? "I tried to shush him so Auntie wouldn't hear, but"—I looked into her eyes with all the sorrow I was feeling—"the one thing he wanted to know was where you were."

And she smiled her Faiza smile.

How could she? If I were her, I'd be howling by now. Not that I hadn't known it, but at that moment the enormity of the gulf between us struck me with dizzying force. Here she was, cherishing the little she could have, while I rebuked the world for not giving me everything I wanted, including happiness for my friend.

She took my hand as if I were the one in need of consoling. "It's okay, Ab, cheer up. I'm fine. Really, I am."

"Oh, Faiza, you're so brave; so strong! I envy you."

"You envy me!" She laughed, and once again I heard an echo of a past conversation.

"You never finished telling me your story, you know!"

"That's true. My story and Asana's."

"What happened after she left?"

Faiza put her arm around me like a mother soothing a fretting child and sat me on the step. She turned her head pan upside down. "Shall I continue?"

I nodded.

Chapter 15

"THE MORNING AFTER ASANA LEFT, WE WERE WOKEN BY THE sound of singing. The women had come to fetch the bride for bathing and for the rites that needed to be performed on this special morning. Luckily, I'd fallen into a deep sleep. I wouldn't have believed I could sleep a wink on such a night, but the work of putting all those pots back quietly on my own and the relief that she'd got away just knocked me out.

"So when the singing women arrived, I awoke together with Auntie Fati in genuine confusion, which, luckily for me, was taken for shock at Asana's absence from the mat next to mine. It took a few seconds to remember everything, and by the time the sweet memory of her flight hit me, I was alert enough to hide it. I jumped up from my mat in alarm, pretending to look for her in the corners of the room.

"Auntie Fati clutched her stomach and had to hurry outside. Her bowels always reacted first to bad news. It was decided that some of the women would walk to the stream to find out if Asana had gone there to bathe herself or to fetch water. This postponed the evil moment, but a sense of dread was taking root. By the time they came back from the stream, shaking their heads, there was more hubbub in the village as the absence of more girls had been discovered. People were beginning to suspect what had happened. It was not the first time a band of girls had run away, but no one wanted to be first to suggest it. Not when Alhaji's bride must be one of the group.

"Auntie was hysterical, tearing at her clothes and ripping off her scarf to expose the short gray hair hardly anyone ever saw. Her sister was sent for and came running to console her. I was asked to prepare porridge for her, which I gladly did, anxious to avoid questions. I needn't have worried; she was too distraught to do anything but weep and wail. She and her sister stayed in the room all day while Uncle went off to face the music. I heard he prostrated himself before Alhaji Brown Teeth, begging for forgiveness.

"Later that day, we saw a police car enter the village. Uncle ran and hid in the bushes. Two police officers from the station at Tolon went to Alhaji's compound. I heard he paid them good money to go and find Asana. Uncle didn't venture home till well after dark, but Auntie never even noticed.

"I wondered what upset her more, the loss of her daughter or of her imminent status as mother-in-law to the most powerful man in the village. But later on, I felt I had done her an injustice, because she never said anything about the missing money. I knew my aunt, and she wouldn't have overlooked a single missing note. She must have had her own thoughts about how it had gone missing and decided to keep quiet over money that might have given her daughter a safe passage to wherever she had fled.

"I wondered if she puzzled over who had taken it, but if she suspected me, she never showed it. She knew how close Asana and I were, and if it had been used for Asana, then it didn't really make any difference who'd done the taking. Sometimes I even thought a part of her was secretly relieved that her daughter had been spared a marriage she dreaded so much.

"Two years passed, and we thought we might see some of the missing girls back for the groundnut harvest, or at least hear they'd been to nearby villages. But it never happened. With Asana in the group, they must have judged it too risky, even after a couple of years. No one wanted to face the wrath of Alhaji Brown Teeth, despite the fact that he'd chosen a replacement bride within a month, frustrated by the incompetence of the district police.

"The girl had already produced a baby, and whenever I saw her, I gave silent thanks to Allah on behalf of Asana and implored Him to keep her safe wherever she was. And that was something I wondered about every day.

"One day, a little girl arrived in our household, about seven years old—a daughter of one of Auntie's other brothers. That made her my cousin, but I'd never met her before. She was older than I'd been when I was given to Auntie. She cried a lot at the beginning because she missed her home, but I tried to comfort her and joke with her, and after a couple of months she was settled and had learned a lot from me about the household chores she had to do. I waited another month and then I asked Auntie if I could go and look for Asana.

" 'Where will you look?' she asked.

" 'In the big city markets. You know that's where they all go, the girls who run away.'

" 'Faiza, do you know where my daughter is?' Auntie was looking straight into my eyes. It was the first time she'd asked me about it directly. I was relieved I could answer truthfully.

" 'No, Auntie Fati, I do not.'

"She dropped her eyes, and I said, 'I miss her too, Auntie. Please let me go and look for her.'

"Rakiya had told me they'd see how far their money took them. They were hoping to get to Accra, but they couldn't be sure, and I had no idea whether they'd been able to make it.

" 'Let me go to Accra, Auntie!'

"She was still for a little while, as if she hadn't heard me. Then she nodded heavily. 'You are growing too now, Faiza. You can also work and earn some money while you are there.' She even gave me the money for the lorry fare to Accra."

"And here you are," I said.

"Yes, but I've not been successful in my mission."

"Not yet. But don't give up, Faiza."

"I don't think she's here, Abena."

"How can you be so sure? Makola's one of the biggest markets in Africa."

"Yes, but we have our networks. I've met other girls from my village here. And from neighboring villages. That's how I was able to find my way around at first and get a place to sleep. We help each other and the new ones when they arrive. But none of them have seen or heard anything of Asana, ever since I arrived. Even some of the food sellers we've been going to—they're my people too, but they haven't heard of any girl like her working in Makola."

"So, what are you going to do?"

"Well," Faiza said, looking directly at me, "I'm almost ready to move on, Abena."

"*What!* You're leaving?"

I'd been so caught up in the world of our friendship

that I'd forgotten—or pushed away—the fact that it must come to an end. And not just because Faiza might be leaving, but because my summer holidays were almost over. In two weeks, I'd be sitting in a classroom again, in the American School. The thought was unreal.

Two young women walked up to the door of the shop, chatting and laughing. We jumped out of the way, and they went in. I sat on the step again and motioned for Faiza to stay.

"Where will you go, Faiza?" I asked her.

"To Kumasi—Kejetia Market. I hear it's even bigger than Makola."

"I've heard that too."

"Most of our girls come to Makola or Kejetia, so if Asana's not here, then that's the next place I must look."

"But what if she's not there either? I mean, she might have moved on, got some other work, even got married!"

"I can only try, Abena. That's what I promised Auntie."

"And...if you don't succeed, will you come back here?"

"I...also promised Auntie I'd go back home if I didn't find Asana." She looked at the ground. "So that is what I must do."

I twisted the yellow duster around my hands. "Faiza, aren't you scared of just...moving from one city to the next like that? D'you know anyone there? D'you have a place to stay?"

She shook her head. "No, but I will find our people in Kejetia too."

"But what if—"

"Abena, fear is what stops us from doing what we want!" She looked me straight in the eye. "I was scared here too, in the beginning, and it all worked out. You see, fear itself is a coward. It can only stop us till we stand up to it, like all bullies."

This friend of mine, I thought yet again, so small and yet so strong.

A banana seller walked by with a tray on her head and a baby in a cloth on her back. I didn't feel like going anywhere, but we could get a "poor man's lunch"— banana and groundnuts. I asked Faiza if she was hungry, and she shook her head. It was past lunchtime now, but

I wasn't either. The woman called out and I signaled no. We watched her walk past in silence. Then Faiza turned to me.

"Abena, I want to thank you. Do you remember that first day we met?"

I nodded. How could I forget?

"Well, from that first time you smiled at me and helped me lift my bowl, I felt at home in this great big, scary Makola Market."

"Me too! It's strange, but that was the moment I really started feeling at home here. Auntie was here and Gifty was here, but still I felt lonely till I met you, Faiza."

We hugged each other to say thank you and other things that were harder to express, like how much a kayayoo from the North and a doctor's daughter from the South had come to mean to each other in less than two months.

"You know," she said as we pulled back, "I would have left already if not for you."

"Really?"

"Remember when Asana told me I was like her twin sister come back?"

I nodded.

190

"You can never replace a beloved person, but the pain gets better when other dear ones come into your life. I'm not sure how to say this, Abena, but... you helped me find myself again after losing her."

"And you helped me find... so many things I didn't even know I didn't have."

We both stared into the market for a few moments. Then Faiza said, "I know your school vacation is almost over, Abena. That's why I am also getting ready to leave."

I took a deep breath to steady my voice. "Will I ever see you again, Faiza?"

She paused, and I felt a sense of helplessness. My school friends and I met on social media and exchanged phone calls and messages even after we'd spent the whole day at school together and would spend the whole of the next day together. But here I was with a friend like none I'd ever had before, who couldn't use any of those things—didn't own a phone, couldn't even write me a letter with pen and paper, and had no post office box to which I could have sent her one. How could we live in such different worlds inside the same country?

We'd never got beyond the basics of reading and writing, and it would take many more lessons for Faiza to be able to compose a letter. She'd also been eager to learn about the world around her, and we'd spent time talking about things I'd learned in history and geography and science classes as well as through TV. I'd never thought of myself as a teacher before. That stuff was just part of school, dreary old school. But now I realized how disconnected one could be—from so much of the world—without it.

"It's not yet time to say goodbye," said Faiza, not quite answering my question. "But it was time to let you know."

At that moment Auntie came out of the shop, seeing off the two women. They weren't loaded down enough to need a kayayoo, but they were singing the shop's praises and promising to come back soon, and Auntie was lapping it all up.

"I should have known you'd be here chatting with your friend," she said to me. Then, to my surprise, she looked at Faiza with something almost approaching warmth and said, "Your friend is soon going back to school, Faiza. I'm sure you'll miss her."

Faiza nodded silently.

"But just because she's not here doesn't mean you

can't keep carrying for us, okay?" And Auntie actually smiled at her.

I couldn't believe my eyes or my ears. She didn't know Faiza would be leaving too, but that wasn't the point. Auntie turned back to me. "I'm going to buy something, so go in and help Gifty."

"Yes, Auntie!" I went back inside shop, beaming, while Faiza melted into her surroundings.

"Where have you been?" asked Gifty. "Let me guess." She rolled her eyes. "Oh yes, with your kayayoo again! Well, it's my turn for a break now. You deal with the customers for a change!"

And she walked out of the shop, holding the door as the next customer walked in.

Chapter 16

THE NEXT MORNING, GIFTY TURNED UP IN A PAIR OF TIGHT JEANS that had a lace-up design showing her skin up the side of each leg, a stretchy new T-shirt in fluorescent orange, and spirally orange earrings.

"It's my birthday!" she announced, cracking her chewing gum, and then, seeing the look on my face, added, "My mother sent me them. Anyway, mind your own business."

"Happy birthday," I said. She looked good, but I was convinced it was no more her birthday than mine. Auntie was not amused, because Gifty had changed into that outfit at the last minute and sneaked into the back of the car before Auntie saw her.

After serving a few customers, Gifty turned to Auntie. "Please, Auntie Lydia, may I go and check if the TV is ready?"

So that was it.

Auntie gave a dismissive flick of her hand, still annoyed with her, but riveted to the virtual opulence of the Dubai shops I'd googled for her an hour ago. She was still confounded if she clicked in the wrong place and her window disappeared, so she was concentrating.

Gifty was out in a flash. She came back smirking with Stephen in tow. He was carrying the TV, and it looked like a new set.

"Good morning, Momee!" he called cheerfully to Auntie Lydia, winking at me.

"Abena, help him put it back," Auntie called in our direction, to Gifty's fresh exasperation.

But this time she refused to be excluded, pushing herself between us and grabbing one end of the TV as if we couldn't possibly manage without a mosquito like her. I smelled a cheap perfume in which she'd doused herself. There'd be no keeping her out of the conversation this time. But Stephen didn't let that deter him.

"So, will you give me your friend's number?" he whispered across to me.

I couldn't help smiling, which infuriated Gifty.

"I can't do that without her permission," I stalled.

"*Permission!*" growled Gifty.

"Oh, come on!" coaxed Stephen as we hoisted the TV onto its stand.

Gifty flicked the switch, and the set flashed to life. "Where's the remote?" she asked, impatient for her telenovelas.

"Oh no, I forgot!" said Stephen.

I stared at him.

"You know what?" He looked pointedly back at me. "Why don't you come with me to the shop to get it?"

Gifty drew a noisy breath, incensed that he should ask me, especially after she'd been the one to go and fetch him.

"Okay!" I said quickly.

I wasn't sure how I was going to keep sidestepping his questions about Faiza, but I was going to see Mike again!

"Auntie, I'm just going to pick up the remote from Blankson's," I said as I bounded out behind Steve.

She nodded absently, absorbed in Dubai finery while popping her snack of mixed popcorn and roasted groundnuts into her mouth.

✦

"I've been trying to find a way to see your friend again," Stephen said as soon as we got outside, as if I didn't know. "But it's so hard to talk in your auntie's shop."

He was walking slowly, but I was speeding up because we were after different things, and I didn't want to fend him off any longer than I had to. The hardest part was holding back from just saying, *Well, you're the one who walked right past her, you idiot!*

I held it together until we got to Blankson's, but he refused to fetch me the remote control unless I gave him my friend's number. Where was their uncle, I wondered, but their shop was much larger than ours and had a full office behind it, and old Blankson clearly gave them a lot of freedom. After all, they were older, and they were boys. They could probably do pretty much what they liked as long as the customers were happy. But surely that couldn't include withholding customers' property from them?

Stephen was so genial about it that I couldn't really be angry, but I was almost ready to say, Look, even if she had a phone, you wouldn't need to call her, because she's right under your nose, but you can't see her because she's a poor kayayoo you wouldn't want to go out with anyway.

Mike came to my rescue. "Chale, why you dey worry my sister like that?" he chided his brother in pidgin. Typical secondary school boys—they all spoke pidgin among themselves to be cool. I wondered which school they went to. One of the boarding ones, most likely. They too would soon be gone from Makola.

"Hello, Abena." He remembered my name without hesitation. "Good to see you here again."

"Same," I said, not quite sure where to look but not wanting to miss too much by looking away either.

"Coming for your plasma TV?" He grinned.

"Not yet," I said, laughing. "Just picking up the remote for the old one." I looked pointedly at his brother.

Mike held it out to me with a look at Stephen that said, Chale, relax! Then he said to me, as if it were the most natural thing in the world, "Steve and I were wondering if you and your friend would like to join us for an ice cream at Milly's when you finish at the shop."

An ice cream at Milly's?

Milly's was a new ice cream parlor by the main road, where people sat under umbrellas amid the smog of Makola and licked at ice cream cones topped with colorful balls that dripped deliciously in the heat. I'd been wanting to go there but had never imagined it happening this way—with this simultaneously delightful and terrifying invitation.

I liked Mike, and he clearly liked me; Faiza liked his brother, and he clearly liked her, but two plus two was just not making four here. No, it was making something like three, an odd and unworkable number for an odd and unworkable situation.

Even if Faiza hadn't melted into a phantom in their world, they were clearly still taking us to be older than we were because of the way we had dressed and acted that day. I'd often been mistaken for being older, but Faiza in her everyday wear actually looked younger than she was. And even if we were able to sneak out for ice cream with two older boys, what kind of conversation could Faiza possibly have with these two? Boutique-speak wouldn't help her here. They'd want girlfriends they could discuss their favorite movies and music with, chat with over the internet, send emoji-filled messages to, show off to their friends. An illiterate girl who walked miles with water or firewood or kaya on her head had no place in that world. I didn't know what to say.

"Thanks, that's nice of you but..."

"Yes?"

I finally found my tongue. "I don't think my friend is coming to the market today."

"But you said she comes here all the time!" said Stephen.

"Yes, but not today," I said firmly. I needed time to think about this.

"What about tomorrow, then?" asked Mike.

I looked at him and wished I could find a way to make it work. But I had to keep my wits about me. I tore my eyes away, over his shoulder. "Okay, you know what—let me ask her and get back to you."

"Fair enough! So, you're working in your auntie's shop over the long vac?"

"Yeah."

"For how long?"

"Just another week. My...long vac is almost over."

I stopped myself from saying *summer holiday*. I wasn't going to let him call me dada bee again. Besides, "long vacation" did make more sense for a country with a rainy season from June till September. I had never really thought about it before.

"So it'll have to be soon," said Stephen.

"Yes, I know. I—I mean, *we*—are also going back to school." I tried to steer the conversation into safer waters. "So, which school are you two at?"

"Motown," Mike said proudly.

Ah, Achimota School, Dad's alma mater. If he was anything like Dad, this should prove a rich diversion. But he bounced the question right back—"And you?"

"The American School."

Ah! A genuine, 100 percent dada ba, his smile said more eloquently than words could ever have done. I was glad I'd said "long vac."

"Your friend too?" Stephen started to ask, but I cut him off and said I really needed to be getting back or Auntie would be angry.

Poor Auntie, I thought, walking back, what an ogre I was making her out to be to these boys. But my thoughts turned out to be prophetic because the moment I entered the shop, I could tell something was wrong. Terribly.

Auntie Lydia was standing by the desk with her arms akimbo. She pointed at me.

"You!" she said, as if I were a stranger. "Come here!"

Chapter 17

I WALKED OVER ON UNSTEADY LEGS, WONDERING WHAT AUNTIE had found out, how much she knew. Faiza coming in? Using her laptop? Our dressing up? Had Gifty talked? Or Auntie Connie? . . . Then I saw that the cash drawer was standing open.

Auntie pointed at it. "Half the money is missing!"

I looked at her, disbelieving.

Behind her, Gifty was smirking, the pained look she'd worn as I exited the shop with Stephen replaced by one of triumph. I clamped a hand over my chest because my heart was trying to jump out. "Auntie Lydia, you think I stole from you?"

"No, silly! Why would you, when your parents are

richer than me? It's your friend I mean—that Hausa girl. The *kayayoo!*" She spat the word out like something disgusting.

I reeled. Faiza was being accused of stealing, being called a 'Hausa girl' in that nasty way, being treated as a nameless kayayoo all over again, when Auntie had actually called her by name, actually spoken to her like a person for the first time, just yesterday.

"Faiza! You think Faiza would steal from you?"

"Why not? She's a poor kayayoo, isn't she? Why wouldn't she take it?"

I wanted to tell Auntie that being poor didn't automatically make people into thieves, but I knew it wouldn't help right now. "Faiza wouldn't do that, Auntie! I know she wouldn't. Please believe me!"

"But I hear you've been bringing her into the shop," she fired with a flourish of her hand. She was watching me keenly. So was Gifty. Traitor!

I should have known the risk was too high. But we'd been having so much fun. I'd let myself get carried away and brushed aside Gifty's jealousy, which had grown steadily, fueled by outrage that the boy she liked now preferred the same wretched kayayoo. And I'd broken

Auntie's rules; there was no denying that. Now I was paying the price for all those follies combined.

Gifty stared brazenly at me.

"Auntie, I'm sorry!" I said. "I shouldn't have gone behind your back."

She nodded sternly.

"But you know Faiza," I implored. "You know she wouldn't do that!"

Auntie stared, unmoved.

"She wouldn't, I tell you. She'd never steal a th—" I faltered, remembering the time she'd stolen money from her own auntie. I tried to cover up, but it was too late.

"You see! You're not even sure yourself. You're her friend, but even you cannot trust her!"

But that was different! She'd done it to help her cousin, to rescue her. Was all stealing bad, no matter what for? I'd never had to think about such things before, and this was not the time to start. My hesitation had already cost too much.

Auntie flung open the door and went outside. She came back with Faiza.

"You this girl!" She pointed at her the way she'd

pointed at me. "Abena brought you into the shop, and you couldn't resist helping yourself to my money!"

Faiza looked bewildered. "No, Madam Lydia." She called her by name for the first time. "Never!"

She looked over at me, and I looked back, tears starting to roll down my cheeks. Auntie addressed us both.

"This is what I get for allowing my niece to befriend a common kayayoo!" She grimaced as if the word injured her mouth. "Ungrateful creature. Get out of my shop! I never want to see you again. Stay away from us! D'you hear?"

"Please, madam," said Faiza. "I can never do such a thing. I did not take your money. I swear it."

"Auntie, please!" I cried.

She stamped her foot as if shooing a stray dog. "I said, *get out!*" she shouted. "Get out of my sight before I call the police!"

Auntie Omotola hurried over from her shop.

Faiza looked at me again, and I looked back at her, helpless. I knew she hadn't taken the money, but I didn't know what more to say or do, because Auntie was acting like someone I didn't know; talking to me like someone she didn't know; treating Faiza like someone none of us knew. I was clueless how to defend her.

Faiza turned and ran away.

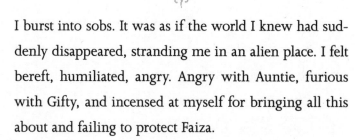

I burst into sobs. It was as if the world I knew had suddenly disappeared, stranding me in an alien place. I felt bereft, humiliated, angry. Angry with Auntie, furious with Gifty, and incensed at myself for bringing all this about and failing to protect Faiza.

My guilt at going behind Auntie's back felt like a wall blocking me from speaking up for Faiza or myself. But still, I should have been able to. I didn't know how, but that was the way I felt; that was what I thought as I stood there by the door of the shop, incoherent, my eyes, nose, whole face streaming, watching Faiza swallowed, in an instant, by the market.

Auntie Omo looked from one face to another, her eyes glistening with tears as they fell on me. She didn't know what had happened between all of us, but she could tell it was bad, and she too felt helpless.

I looked at Gifty again, but this time she turned away.

Auntie Omo held out her arms to me, but I couldn't stay in this place.

I ran into the market, ignoring Auntie's call, looking for Faiza; but with that small head start, she had disappeared.

I turned, in which direction I hardly knew, searching for her anywhere, everywhere—in shops, outside Blankson's, at My Redeemer Lives Hair and Beauty Parlor, at the open-air restaurant, in the little alley where we'd removed our fine feathers; in all the places we'd been together.

She was nowhere to be found.

I looked and looked for what seemed like hours and probably was. But she truly had vanished into her surroundings as completely as she always did, and although I was always the one who could find her, this time she was invisible to me too.

I trudged around the vast market till my feet hurt and I was sweating and tired. I still hadn't found Faiza, but I couldn't bring myself to go back to the shop. I couldn't face Auntie, I couldn't stand to look at Gifty, and above all I couldn't face myself. I felt as if I wanted to run away from myself.

Unable to walk another step, I came to a standstill at the back of a wholesale shop and flopped onto a little culvert among empty cartons and crates, almost hidden by them. I barely noticed the stench from the drain. I sat staring into space, feeling like Asana must have felt when she'd wished herself away from something she couldn't face.

I knew I wasn't going to find Faiza. And I knew I would probably never see her again. Never had I imagined that we would say goodbye—or rather, not say goodbye—in such a way. I hid my head in my lap and folded my arms around it, shutting out the world.

I have no idea how long I sat there like that, but the next thing I knew, someone was tapping me on the elbow. I looked up and saw, to my shock, that it was dark. I'd dozed off. The owner of the store was locking up and had spotted me outside, among the boxes.

"What's wrong?" he asked. "Are you ill?"

"I'm fine," I said mechanically, feeling far from it. I was dazed and hadn't eaten since breakfast, but I couldn't call the gnawing feeling in my stomach hunger, because I had no appetite, and it just blended in with all the other things gnawing at me. I straightened out my crumpled skirt, wet down the front, and looked at my watch. It was time to go.

Auntie Lydia and Gifty were waiting in the shop, though it was an hour past closing time. Auntie looked at me as I entered, with feeling in her eyes, but asked nothing. I could tell she'd been worried. Gifty and I didn't even look at each other. I collected my things, and Auntie locked up behind us. This time there'd be no Faiza to accompany us to the car with the laptop bag slung over her small shoulder.

As the car moved through the darkening streets, I stared out the window, unseeing. I wondered if somewhere Faiza was also staring out of a darkening window as the city receded behind her.

Chapter 18

I WENT BACK HOME THE NEXT DAY. I WAS SUPPOSED TO HAVE stayed with Auntie a week longer, but I had a fever and my head hurt, and she wanted to hand me over to Dad before it got any worse.

It was a relief for everyone. I didn't want to be with her or Gifty anymore, and I didn't feel like going to Makola ever again. At least I had a good excuse not to move in with my cousins. I couldn't face that right now. As for Faiza, I couldn't even bear to think about her. It hurt too much, like a headache that made you have to hold your head still.

Dad was still busy at the clinic, and Mom was due back next week with little Kwesi, but I was happy to be alone for most of the day. Dad took me to his clinic for a blood test and said I had malaria. I had had it many times before, but this was the worst it had ever made me feel. My head was pounding and my teeth chattered with cold, while my body felt as hot to the touch as if I were about to burst into flames. Dad gave me medicine and told me to stay in bed. Dinah took care of me, carrying trays up and down all day. Pierre made all my favorite things, like lasagna and potato pancakes and chocolate mousse and apple pie with custard, but I could barely eat. Dad came back from the clinic during his lunch breaks and closed early to come home to "his most important patient," as he called me. He would eat his supper by my bedside, trying to coax me to eat too.

I slept and watched cable TV all day, needing to escape from my own thoughts and from myself. In between, I just stared in an out-of-focus way at the silky purple fabric of my curtains, not really seeing them.

The fever was gone after two days, but my appetite was still not back. Dad saw my untouched supper tray when he came up to my room that evening, carrying his own. He lifted the lids and frowned at the limp French fries, the congealed chicken stew, the furrowed skin on the custard. He took the tray outside.

"It's freezing in here," he said, coming back in. "Can I turn the AC off?"

I shrugged, huddled under the duvet. He picked up the remote from my night table and switched it off. Then he drew the curtains and opened the windows. A fragrance of moist earth blew in, mingled with the jasmine trailing over my window roof cover. Rain always brought out the scent of those flowers. I heard a light drizzle outside, and I breathed in deep. I'd had no idea what the weather was.

Dad came and reached for my hands. He gripped them over the bedclothes. His own felt warm and steady, like an anchor in my wobbly world.

"Abee, is something bothering you? I expected you to be more, you know...perky by now."

I looked away, and he could see he was right. "Dearest, talk to me, please. What is it?"

I saw the worry in his eyes. Yes, I'd tell him, or he might fear something even worse.

"Dad, I lost a friend," I began, and tears came immediately. I pulled my hands from his and covered my face.

"What?" He was alarmed. "Who? Surely, you don't mean..."

"No, nobody died," I said, thinking that it was not only people who could die. It was joy and hope and dreams too. For the first time in days, I allowed myself to imagine Faiza, and I thought of how I would never see her again. My voice caught in a sob; my throat burned, and my whole face began to melt down the way it had on that unthinkable day.

Dad fetched the box of tissues from my dresser. "Oh, sweetheart!" He pulled my hands gently away and wiped my face. I clamped the tissues to my face and tried to tell him I was all right, but my voice had deserted me.

Dad sat on the bed and put his arms around me. "It's okay," he murmured. "It's okay; it's okay."

He patted me gently on the back, and I shook us both with sobs till I was able to find my voice again.

"Oh God, I'm sorry, Dad," I whispered.

"Abee, just tell me what happened, please."

With my head on his shoulder, I told him about

214

Faiza at last. "She was a kayayoo," I said, "in Makola Market."

He pulled away to look at me. "You made friends with a kayayoo?"

I grabbed more tissues from the box and busied myself wiping my face and blowing my nose, making a great business of it so I could avoid his eyes, but he lifted my chin with his finger and made me look right into them.

"Abee, that's fantastic!"

I looked at him closely for the first time since he'd come in, and he was all crinkly around the eyes with delight. I wasn't sure what I had expected, but...not this. A load fell off me right that moment.

"Most kids like you would think they were too good to be friends with a kayayoo!"

I knew what he meant, but I actually felt almost as if Faiza had been too good for me. Like so much about her, it seemed the wrong way around when you looked at it in the "normal" world. But I was starting to wonder what normal really meant.

"Tell me more about her!" Dad's face was like a kid's.

All the words I'd kept trapped for two months

suddenly tried to rush out at the same time. "Oh, Dad, she was just the most amazing girl!"

He kicked off his slippers and leaned back against the wall with his knees up, arms folded around them, looking at me. "What was it you liked so much about her?"

"She never pretended to be anything she wasn't. And she was so smart, Dad. You wouldn't have believed it."

"Oh yes, I would."

"And so fun! She had this great big smile, and she'd say, 'Abba!' and 'Woi!' and 'Mbo!' and she was always up for trying new things, learning new things, and she was just...my kind of person."

Dad nodded as I spoke. "She sounds amazing."

The wind billowed the curtains into the room, and I heard it rustle through the trees outside.

"She was just so different from anyone I've ever met! I mean, she farmed okro, of all things. And she loves okro flowers. Can you imagine?"

"Ah, but they're beautiful! Like fluffy yellow pinwheels, purple on the inside."

"That's what she said! She taught me so many things, Dad."

"So." He took my hand gently. "What happened with Faiza?"

I held on to his hand and fixed my eyes on the peach and purple unicorns flying over my duvet. "Dad, I disobeyed Auntie and brought Faiza into the shop when she was out. I wanted to show her the internet. She'd never seen it or even touched a computer. I showed her the dinosaurs and the pyramids and the planets."

"I bet she enjoyed that!"

"Oh God, you should have seen her! But this week, some money went missing from the shop. Gifty told Auntie about me bringing Faiza in, and Auntie blamed it on her."

Dad sighed. "I can see why you wanted to show your friend the internet, Abee. But you know you shouldn't have broken your auntie's rules, don't you?"

"Yes. It was bad of me and I apologized, but, Dad, I know she didn't take the money! Auntie was acting like she must have just because she was poor, but I know she'd never do such a thing, no matter what."

"I believe you."

"But Auntie didn't. She sacked her from the shop! She disgraced her. She even threatened to call the police!

I didn't know what to do, Dad." Tears came back into my eyes. "I didn't even get a chance to say goodbye."

"I'm so sorry, sweetie. Sounds like it was all a dreadful misunderstanding. Would you like me to speak to your auntie?"

"But it wasn't a misunderstanding! Not the way you mean. You see...Auntie has her own ideas about people. She kept calling Faiza a Hausa girl even though she's a Dagomba—but in a way that made it sound like an insult."

"That's not right." Dad frowned.

"Faiza's the smartest girl I've ever met, Dad. But Auntie acted like she was nothing, deserved nothing, just because she was poor and came from the North. I'd asked her if I could show Faiza the internet, but she said no, that Faiza would carry off her laptop in her head pan. That's what she said! She and Gifty laughed about it."

Dad got up and went over to the window. He gathered up the billowing curtains, looped the tiebacks around them on either side, and fixed them neatly on their hooks. He turned slowly back to me. "I'm sorry to say this, Abee, but when people behave like that, it's just themselves they're insulting, because they're showing their own ignorance."

"That's what I meant!" I threw off the duvet and sat up. "It's like she didn't *want* to understand."

Dad sighed again. "Adults make mistakes too, Abee. It wasn't right for her to say those things and to treat your friend the way she did."

"I know, but she wouldn't listen to me."

"Of course not." Dad walked back to the bed, picked up the juice box from my night table, and poured out two glasses. He handed me one. "I'm sorry you had to go through that, sweetheart. There's a lot I respect about your aunt, and I thought being with her would be a good change for you, but—"

"Oh, but don't be sorry, Dad. You were right!"

"What?"

"Why d'you think I still wanted to stay at Auntie's after Brit and Tiff came? It was tough at first, but it started to feel like . . . a different kind of home, and that made me feel like a different kind of person. Not just her house—the market too. It gave me the chance to meet Faiza. And even Auntie herself—she's not my favorite person right now, but . . . I know she has her good sides."

"She's been calling every day to ask how you are."

I sighed. "I still can't believe how it ended, but... Dad, I wouldn't have missed it for the world."

"Aw, Abee!" He hugged me again. "I'm so glad."

"And I'm hungry!" I said over his shoulder.

"Praise the Lord! Shall I ask Dinah..."

"I feel like eating kelewele. From—"

"Labone Junction!" He jumped up. "I'll go myself. To make sure it's fresh."

I'd never seen anyone move as fast as my dad did that evening, getting me the first food I had asked for since I got home.

Chapter 19

THE SKY WAS LIGHTENING TO PINK OUTSIDE MY WINDOW WHEN I woke up the next morning. I wasn't usually up this early, but my sleeping patterns were messed up because I'd been sleeping so much during the day. I switched on my phone, and an email title popped up on my lock screen. *Oh, Jesus!* The competition!

I feverishly opened my email, trying to damp down my hopes in advance. Of course I wasn't going to place; it was going to be one of those extra-polite emails that told you how fierce the competition had been, how excellent the quality of entries, how hard the choice for the judges, how much they'd enjoyed your submission—but, alas, it wasn't exactly what they were looking for—and how fervently they urged you to keep on writing and wished you all the best for your future endeavors. I tried to take in the whole email at a glance and home in on those key words to end the agony in one stroke.

"Oh my God!" I shrieked. I hadn't placed overall, but I had come in second in the Urban Bustle category for my article on Makola Market.

Dad came running, hair uncombed, shirt half buttoned. "Abee!"

"It's okay, Dad; good news!"

He put his hand up to his chest and panted. "Don't scare me like that!"

I hadn't told anyone but Faiza about the competition. I hadn't wanted to disappoint them, but Faiza got that it was a long shot and could cheer me on without my feeling any pressure. The way Dad was carrying on now, you'd have thought I'd won the whole thing. But I was thrilled too. Second place in a subcategory was something to be proud of in an international online competition. The prizewinners were from all over the world—India, Australia, Singapore, the UK, the US, and other African countries too. But I was the only one from

West Africa. The prize was an ebook token and publication in an online journal. Seeing my name on the screen among the winners was like another prize.

"We'll celebrate when I get back from work!" said Dad.

I longed to tell Faiza, but I video-called Mom, and she was even more excited than Dad. "Mo-m!" I rolled my eyes when she started sniffling. "It's not the Nobel Prize!"

"Oh, Abee! And for an article on Makola Market. Your auntie will be so proud!"

I thought of Auntie Lydia. If the unthinkable hadn't happened, she'd be sending Gifty out for Guinness right now. And Malta or Coke for us. Dancing a jig and saying what a brilliant niece she had. I'd go and find Faiza and she'd say, *Mbo! What did I tell you?*

How could the world just change in an instant like that?

"Yeah," I said to Mom, "sure." And before she could say anything else, I asked about my little brother. She showed me him sleeping peacefully in a Moses basket with his knitted white cap over his eyebrows. He was starting to fill out. His skin looked as tautly fresh as newly ripe fruit, and he twitched his mouth in his sleep. I wanted to reach out and touch him. "When are you baaack?" I asked plaintively.

"Just over a week now, darling. It'll fly—you'll see."

I stayed in bed most of day because I still felt wobbly every time I got up.

The news of the competition made me start writing in my diary again. But after a while, I realized I wasn't writing to the diary anymore. I was writing to Faiza. Sharing the news and just catching her up on my life. The more I wrote, the more I felt it—hope wasn't dead; dreams weren't dead. I wasn't sure how, but the same way she had known she was going to help Asana escape, I knew we'd find each other again. One day. And when we did, it would be easier to catch up this way. Because she would want every detail, and so would I.

※

Dad came back earlier than usual from work, with a bottle of sparkling grape juice and a cream cake with gold frosting that had "CONGRATULATIONS!" iced around it.

"I'll take you out for dinner when you're better, for a proper celebration," he said.

I wished we could do it now, but I was still trembly on my feet. At least I'd got out of my pajamas. To make our dinner a little festive, I'd put on a full-skirted dress that Auntie Lydia's seamstress had sewn for me in a floral print. We had it in my room again, but this time on the wicker furniture in the alcove near the door.

I told Dad how sick I was of being sick. He said I was weak because the malaria parasite had killed off my red blood cells. That was why he'd asked Pierre to prepare kontomire stew, made of rich green taro leaves. Iron-rich foods would bring my strength back, he said. I thought of the soups Faiza had introduced me to. I bet they'd be good for me too.

"Dad, have you heard of a leaf called 'bra'?" I did my best to roll the r as Faiza had, so it wouldn't sound like "come" in Twi or "underwear" in English.

"Yup." He nodded, to my amazement.

"How do you know it?"

"From the North."

"You've been?"

He smiled. "I worked there."

How hadn't I known this? He laughed at the look on my face. "You never asked, did you, you little southerner!"

I pulled a face at him. But it was true; I'd hardly ever even thought about the North till I'd met Faiza.

I cut a piece off my slice of boiled yam and used my knife to pile kontomire stew onto it. It was good, but not like Auntie Lydia's. The oil, for starters—Auntie was such a stickler for palm oil. She had a special place at the market where she bought her zomi, the best grade of it—thick and orange, with a scent that made your mouth water. This stew also had less chili pepper and was missing the flavors Auntie's had. She'd grind up dried shrimp, tiny dried fish, seedpods, and other seasonings whose names I didn't even know in English. I'd grown used to hotter, spicier food at her place, and to eating most things with my fingers because we all did—not just fufu and banku, like at home. Everything was somehow tastier that way. I could do it now if I wanted; I knew Dad wouldn't mind. But it wasn't the same.

"I was a new doctor, and they posted me to the Tamale Regional Hospital," he said. "Talk about in at the deep end! It was before you were born. Even before I met your mother."

"Tamale! Yeah, now that you say it, I remember you talking about it. But it didn't really mean anything to me back then."

"Thank God for Faiza!"

"So, what was it like?"

"Hot as hell—sure puts the "Sahara" in "sub-Saharan"! Challenging too, especially at the hospital—medical facilities and supplies next to zero, but I learned to do a lot with a little." He stroked his beard, eyes far away in the past. "It toughened me up, I can tell you."

I heard her again—*When life is tough, you have to be tough.*

"They're still short of doctors now. Medicines too. Back then I even learned to use some of the traditional remedies people used locally. You'll try anything when you need to save a life."

We were done with dinner. Dad cut the cake and popped the sparkling grape juice. He filled a couple of wine-glasses, and they frothed and fizzed at the top.

"Congrats, Abee," he toasted me. "I'm so proud of the person you're becoming."

"Not a dada ba anymore, then?" I grinned.

"But still my girl, I hope."

"Always." I clinked my glass against his.

The bubbles tickled my nose as I drank. Dad passed me some cake. I was pretty full, but it tasted of chocolate and vanilla, and I finished the whole slice. My appetite was definitely back to normal. I set my plate on the table and leaned back against the peach-colored cushions, patting my tummy as I put my legs up.

Dad leaned back too. "You know, Abee, my years in the North were what made me specialize in tropical medicine. The knowledge of plants and herbs among people there, especially in the villages . . . it just blew my mind.

"Yeah, Faiza told me they use charcoal for stomachache."

"That's just the beginning. They even have their own bone-setting techniques."

"Wow!"

"I loved it there. It was tough at first, but the people were so warm. The way they opened up their homes to me—I've never known such hospitality. And their food! My colleagues took me home on the weekends, and their mothers and wives cooked for me and, oh God, the TZ and the soups! With all those fabulous green leaves—alefu, ayoyo, bra..."

"There you go! I had bra soup at the market!"

"With groundnut paste?"

"Sooo yummy!"

"And can you guess which plant those leaves come from? *Hibiscus sabdariffa*." Dad leaned over and topped up my glass. "The sorrel plant."

"Sorrel?"

"The one that makes the red drink; you know—bissap."

"Oh! We were always drinking it in the market. They called it 'sobolo' there."

"It's made from the calyx of the flowers."

"So the leaves are the 'bra' in bra soup?" It felt almost like being with Faiza again—that discovery of things that had been around all along.

Dad nodded. "Both insanely good for you and with healing properties too. And you know what else is a type of hibiscus? Your okro plants! That's why their flowers are so pretty. They look just like sorrel flowers, by the way."

"You learned all this up there?"

"And from researching what I heard. I never stopped asking questions. From colleagues, friends, patients, the market women..."

"And Faiza thought I was bad!"

I wished I'd spoken to Dad about these things a long time ago. And I wished I could have told Faiza that my dad had lived up north. "Woi!" she'd have said.

"But I learned a lot as a child too. You know I grew up in the village—farming okro, just like your friend!"

"What?" I'd known my father was born in the village, but...it hadn't really meant much till now.

"My father abandoned my mother when I was little," said Dad. "We wore rags and never had enough food, but I worked hard on the farm and was forever asking questions, so my mother begged her brother to send me to school. I lived with him and worked on his cocoa farm, and he supported me till I completed secondary school and won a scholarship to study medicine."

"Wow, Dad! I'm proud of you!" I raised my glass. "Here's to you."

We clinked glasses, and he smiled till his eyes crinkled up again. "Don't ever let anyone make you feel bad for befriending a village girl, Abee. Because, remember, your father is a village kid too."

Chapter 20

I WAS BACK ON MY FEET TO GREET MOM AND LITTLE KWESI WHEN they arrived at last. He was all baby sounds and smells. And he got so excited every time I played with him, flailing his arms and legs about. I couldn't put him down. I'd wanted a brother or sister for years, but Mom had suffered from poor health because of asthma, and I'd grown used to being the only child.

She was amazed how much I'd grown over the holidays. "We're two women in the house now!" she said over breakfast the next morning. Kwesi was asleep upstairs, so we'd started catching up.

She had a short new Afro and was a bit thinner than

usual, which surprised me, although, unlike Auntie Lydia, she'd never been able to keep weight on. She said it was all going into feeding Kwesi. She looked altogether younger, which was kind of unnerving—like having some other girl walking around the house. But the way she fussed over me soon made her back into Mom again.

She presented me with my new laptop after breakfast, she and Dad both beaming. It was so beautiful, I couldn't believe it was mine. She'd bought some special design and publishing software as a gift after hearing about my performance in the competition—"We must equip the first journalist in the family!"

She was still so excited. She'd told all the family in the UK and the US and all her friends about my article. You'd have thought I was world-famous. But I was psyched too. It felt like the sky was the limit with all this new stuff. Mom even knew bits of my article by heart— "The kayayoo carriers of Makola Market may seem like a faceless band of workers," she recited, "but they are young girls like any others, with their own stories, hopes, and dreams."

"Oh, Abee, the way you wrote about those kayayei— it was my favorite bit."

"Really?" It was hard to stop smiling, hearing her quote me.

"Sweetheart, you observe with so much feeling. You just brought that whole market to life! What did your Auntie Lydia think? She must have been over the moon!"

"Yeah, she was... pretty happy." I avoided her eyes and Dad's. "Mom, can you show me how this software works?"

"Hmm... your dad might be a better bet for that. So... everything went okay, then—with your aunt?"

"Yeah. Sure. Fine." I got up from the table and headed for the stairs. "I'll tell you more about it later," I called over my shoulder. "I'm going to set up my laptop!"

"I'll have to call to thank her for having you. You did that yourself already, right?"

I ran quickly out of earshot and up the stairs. I didn't want to bother her with the Faiza matter now; she needed to settle back home with Kwesi. There'd be time enough for that later. I doubted Auntie would say anything just yet. My illness had really alarmed her, Dad had told me. He wouldn't tell either, till I was ready.

Mom wasn't the only one who needed to settle. Having a baby in the house was a new life for us all. There was a changing table in the corridor, a baby bathtub in the bathroom, a crib in Mom and Dad's room, a Moses basket in the living room, and rattles and soft toys all over the place. He was awake during the night and asleep during the day, so Mom and Dad were yawning all the time, and we had to be quiet when he napped, which was much of the day, and he basically ruled the place, breaking up whatever we were doing with his cries when he was hungry, needed his diaper changed, or whatever else, whether we could figure it out or not. It was lucky for him he was so cute, with those round cheeks growing plumper every day.

There was more settling down to be done the following week, when I went back to school, but it happened fast, with all the busyness, timetables, routines, and familiar faces. Now that Lucy was gone, I didn't have anyone in particular to hang out with, but I didn't notice it as much as I would have before Faiza came along. Makola seemed worlds away now, and the disaster of my last day there was fast receding, but what never left my memory was Faiza herself. As I was reunited with my friends, it struck me that something was missing from our interactions and how I'd never noticed it before. They were fun and part of my daily life, but there was no one I could be myself with the way I had with her.

In English class, Ms. Faraday announced that we had an award-winning junior journalist in our midst, and the whole class clapped. It was she who had told us about the competition, but I hadn't told her I was going for it—I hadn't even planned to at first, so she took me by surprise. It turned out a couple of my classmates had also entered but hadn't placed. So, the applause felt good even though it made me a bit self-conscious.

Ms. Faraday asked us to talk about what we'd done during our summer holidays. Most of my schoolmates had been abroad. Helena Owusu talked about shopping on Oxford Street—not the Osu version, the one in London. Alex Ampofo told us about some huge aquarium in Dubai and went on about sharks swimming over his head. Janice Mensah had been in Toronto with relatives and talked loudly in her newly fortified American accent about celebrating her birthday in a revolving restaurant at the top of a tower. Julie Clark talked about all the places she'd been to with her boyfriend. Actually, she just wanted to talk about the boyfriend—Brad.

The other foreign kids had also been back home or to exotic resorts all over the world—Caribbean islands, the Maasai Mara, the Maldives. When I said I'd spent the holiday with my aunt in Makola Market, there were a few giggles. But I didn't care. I'd been abroad on holiday many times before, but this long vac at Makola had been the most memorable of my life.

I knew that virtually no one in my class would have been there, not even the Ghanaian children. Like me before the vacation, they and their parents shopped at the malls, supermarkets, and boutiques and would find the markets too rough and chaotic. They might send their house help instead.

Ms. Faraday would be lost in Makola too. There was no system she would recognize, and prices would triple as soon as they saw and heard her. I had no idea what she did in her spare time, but most of the Americans I knew hung out with other Americans and expats. They bought their food at the commissary and never went far beyond Osu for their shopping and restaurants. It had never really struck me before, but they had a fair bit in common with rich Ghanaians.

I described Makola in detail, and Ms. Faraday nodded delightedly. She'd read my article, so she had some good questions. The others joined in,

"So, you can get huge snails there?" asked Alex Ampofo.

I told them about the traditional medicine section, where you could get dried chameleons and other weird and wonderful stuff. I suspected that Alex and his cronies would soon be visiting Makola. Some of the girls were interested to hear about my auntie's shop and all the fabrics and clothes and makeup one could buy in the market, so much cheaper than in the malls and Osu shops.

One of the things Ms. Faraday had asked us to mention was "new people you met." So I told them about Faiza. I knew they might not have seen kayayei, because they didn't go to markets, and they might not understand the word "kayayoo," so I tried to find another way to put it.

"She was a kaya girl," I said.

"A kaya girl?" Ms. Faraday asked, sounding the r with her American accent, while several of my classmates echoed my own question from two months ago: "A kaya-what?"

I explained to them what a kayayoo was and talked about the North—the things I'd learned from Faiza, the lives of girls like her in the city markets. I had a lot to say because of all the research I'd done. It was so different from everyone else's account of the holidays that they all listened quietly. When I was done, Ms. Faraday thanked me for teaching us all so many new things about the country in which we lived.

"Why is it that people here aren't interested in the North?" I asked Mom and Dad over Sunday lunch.

I was still mulling over my class's reaction to my account of the holidays—how little they'd known, how little I'd known before I met Faiza.

It was so good to have the family together again, our new addition sitting grandly in his rocker on the chair between Mom and me. His eyes followed as my hand moved between my bowl and my mouth, and he made increasingly excited movements and noises, poking out his little tongue as if the food were getting closer to him each time. He was breaking my heart, but there was no way I could give him fufu and palm nut soup, though I might've been tempted to sneak him a taste if Mom hadn't been there.

"Why are you interested?" she asked.

"I learned a bit about it in the market. You know— researching my article."

She turned to Dad—"You must be pleased!"—and back to me—"Careful now, you'll make him nostalgic for his footloose and fancy-free days up there!"

Dad smiled, pinching a large piece of fufu off the mound in his bowl. "That's a good question, Abee, though it's not just in Ghana that southerners aren't interested in the North. He made an indent in his fufu, gathered some soup into it, and swallowed it. "Have you ever had a good look at the map of West Africa?"

"I guess." I shrugged. "Why?"

Kwesi gave a tentative yelp as I put another piece of fufu into my mouth, arching up against his rocker. Mom cooed at him and set the rocker moving with one hand, eating faster with the other. He whimpered and quieted down.

Dad licked his fingers, wiped his hand with a napkin, and pushed back his chair.

"It's okay, he'll settle down," said Mom.

"Actually," said Dad, "I was going..." He trailed off.

I knew he wanted to fetch the atlas from the bookshelf in the living room. That was so Dad. Every question was a chance for a lesson, no matter what else was going on.

"No books at the table!" Mom shook her head.

"I could open Google M—" I began.

"No phones at the table!" Mom shot me a warning glance.

Dad and I grinned at each other. *Welcome back, Mom,* we were both saying in our heads.

She chuckled. "Someone needs to get you two back to civilization."

Kwesi started to fuss for real, thrashing his legs like he was trying to ride a bicycle. Mom called Dinah to take him. Dinah unbuckled him from the rocker and, cooing, put him over her shoulder and walked around, half bouncing, to soothe him. It didn't work, so she took him outside so that Mom could finish her food in peace, but we heard him crying through the French windows. Mom ate like she was in a race, trying to ignore the sound, but it grew into a steady wail. I'd never seen her eat like this before.

"I can't stay ahead of this guy's appetite." She took big spoonfuls of her soup, stood up, and gulped down the rest of her water. "Abee wasn't like this. Boys!"

She went outside, and he yelled at the top of his lungs as soon as he saw her. The minute we heard them climb the stairs, Dad went for the atlas. I pushed my bowl to one side, keeping my soup-coated fingers inside it. Kwesi's cries receded as Dad placed the atlas on the table, opened to a map of West Africa. "Look how straight some of these borders are."

I traced them in sharp strokes with my free hand— Mauritania, Mali, Niger, Chad. "It's like someone drew them with a ruler!"

"That's more or less what they did."

"Who?"

"The colonizers—England, France, Portugal. They didn't care; they were just vying with one another for territory. They drew borders through ethnic groups, clans, villages, even through homes, throwing different peoples together into colonies. And those colonies became nations."

"Hang on..." I was getting confused.

"Okay." Dad snapped the atlas shut and sat on the chair next to me, holding up a forefinger. "Imagine you woke up one day and your house here in Labone and your cousins' house in Trasacco were in two different countries."

"What?"

"And you and your cousins had to learn new languages, different from each other, because the people who'd split you up were rivals, and each wanted you to speak their language. And imagine they told you that your school, the American School, was part of your new country but that you'd need a passport and a visa to go to your cousins' place."

"No way!" I helped myself to more soup. Auntie Lydia had sent it, and it was fantastic—full of smoked fish and crabs. It felt a bit odd enjoying something so much when it came from her, but I'd missed food that tasted like this.

"Not really. Take the Ɛwɛ people. Our eastern border split them between Ghana and Togo. There are villages in the Volta Region where people speak English on one side of the border and French on the other—in the same village!"

"What! But they still speak Ɛwɛ too, right?"

"Thankfully, yes.

"And in the North, Dagbanli?"

"Yes, but it's only one of many northern languages."

I fished a bright red crab out of the soup pot. "Dad, is Hausa another of the northern languages?"

"Yes, but strictly speaking, it's not indigenous to Ghana. The Hausas came in from other countries, mainly Nigeria." He was smiling, watching me tackle the crab. "Aren't you afraid of those things?"

"Not anymore!" I cracked the shell and scooped out the white flesh. "Gifty taught me how to eat them."

"Carry on!" He chuckled.

"So, then, why was Auntie always calling Faiza a Hausa girl?"

"Hausas have settled all over West Africa, especially in the northern parts, and their language is spoken all over the subregion—it's become what people call a lingua franca. So a lot of southerners just use 'Hausa' to mean everything northern, basically."

"It wasn't nice how they said it, though."

"Like we said the other day, Abee, people have all kinds of notions about people who are different from them. And the sad thing is, those notions can be more real to them than what's before their eyes and ears. Few southerners ever go up north, so they just stick to what's in their heads about it."

"You sound like Faiza!" I licked soup off my fingers. "Something she said about looking without seeing."

Dad sighed. "She's young, but she's felt it already. You see, Abena, ethnic groups in the North and South of Ghana are quite distinct from each other. Colonization brought them together into one country, but their cultures, languages, and religions can be very different."

"That's true. Faiza is Muslim." I picked up my side plate, slid the fish bones and crab shells into my bowl, and covered it up. "You know what's wild, though, Dad?

She's the most different friend I've ever had, but the easiest to understand. When we were talking and laughing, none of that stuff made any difference. We didn't even remember it."

"It's not wild at all. Our countries—the whole world—would be much stronger if everyone could be that way."

Chapter 21

My life was settling back into a routine, and it was a calming feeling. The sadness of losing Faiza felt like something that would always be with me, but talking things through with Dad had made the pain less raw. And I had my mom back, and a new brother.

Little Kwesi could be a pain sometimes, but he always managed to melt my heart with his smiles. I played with him after school, but I also enjoyed it whenever I had the chance to be alone with Mom and Dad again. After supper, Dad and I would chat or watch TV in the living room while Mom gave Kwesi his bedtime feed. When she was done, she'd come and cuddle up next to me on the sofa.

One evening, a couple of weeks after she had come

home, I decided I was ready to tell her about Faiza. I was lying on the sofa with my head in her lap. Dad came in from the kitchen with a tray—ice cream for all of us, scooped into sundae glasses, with a wafer stuck in each. He'd even remembered to sprinkle chocolate powder over mine.

I propped myself up against Mom and took a spoonful. It tasted like joy, creamed and frozen. Dad never forgot my favorite flavors. I let a second spoonful melt on my tongue, and then I balanced the glass on my lap and cleared my throat.

"Mom," I said, "there's something I need to tell you."

"Oh?" She looked at me, then at Dad, then at the look that passed between the two of us. She stuck her spoon into her ice cream and set her glass on a side table. "I'm listening."

I told her everything, right up to the terrible day when Faiza and I had not said goodbye. This time there were no tears when I talked about it, which was a relief because I didn't want to alarm her. She had enough crying on her hands with Kwesi.

When I was done, she reached for her ice cream, now mostly melted, and absently took a spoonful. Then she said, "My God, Abee, I can't believe you didn't tell me any of this before!"

"You had a lot on your plate too, Mom."

I saw reproach struggle with pride on her face. "You've done a lot of growing up, my girl," she said, "and I'm so sorry you went through all that."

We talked about it for the rest of the evening: my whole stay with Auntie Lydia, my friendship with Faiza, and the way things had turned out. Like Dad, she felt I'd been wrong to go behind Auntie's back, but she believed that Faiza was innocent. "I wonder who took that money," she murmured, stroking my hair.

"Good question, Mom."

I surprised myself by saying that, because there was no doubt in my mind—Gifty had taken it.

In a subconscious way I'd known it all along, but reading back in my diary, there were so many clues. And my photos just backed them up. I'd taken a whole bunch just of the shop, the fabrics, the customers, Auntie, Gifty...and I'd had time to look through them while I was recovering. They brought her right back to life in my mind—her studied facial expressions; her way around people—always ready with disclaimers and accusations; how she loved handling money, even from customers she hadn't served. And reading my diary entries in one stretch made me realize how things had begun to build up in a way I couldn't see at the time. It all fell into place now.

That afternoon when Auntie had been chatting to us outside the shop and had actually been nice to Faiza for the first time, Gifty had been alone inside for a few minutes—plenty of time to take the money out of the drawer. She'd probably heard Auntie finally warm to Faiza, which wouldn't have helped. It was bad enough that I preferred Faiza, but, worst of all, the boy Gifty had fallen for now had a crush on Faiza, instead of her. It was enough to make you feel sorry for Gifty, really—if only she hadn't brought it all on herself.

As soon as I'd gone back inside, she'd gone out, telling me it was my turn to look after the customers for a change. She hadn't said where she was going, but I now realized she'd gone shopping with the money—for the showy outfit she'd worn the next day, claiming it was her birthday. Then she'd convinced Auntie to let her go to Blankson's.

It was so clear now—it had all been a scheme to impress Stephen, whom she'd determined to get her claws into the minute she heard him ask for Faiza. And when, despite her best efforts, he barely noticed her, she had to do something about it—put that blasted kayayoo in her place once and for all; get her out of the way at last. I still remembered the look she'd given me as Stephen and I left together for Blankson's.

As soon as we were gone, she'd have cooked up an excuse to get Auntie to notice the theft, and then told her I'd brought Faiza into the shop, knowing that could only mean one thing to her.

It was the neatest revenge on both of us. She knew Auntie would rather blame a poor kayayoo from the North than her own relative, no matter how she treated her. And Gifty also knew I couldn't stand up to Auntie after disobeying her and bringing Faiza into the shop. She held all the cards, Gifty did, and I'd played right into her hands.

It seemed absurd to shield her now, but we'd lived and worked together for two months and somehow managed to figure out our own peculiar way of getting along. If there'd been no Faiza, we might even have been some kind of friends. A part of me did feel sorry for her—that she couldn't just stop all her wannabe ways and be comfortable in her own skin, the way Faiza was. That must have been what she'd envied most about Faiza, because it was what made other people love her. But that was exactly the problem—Gifty trampled so readily on other people's feelings that it was easy to forget she had any of her own. I'd been so crushed for Faiza when Stephen walked right past her, but I'd never wondered what it must have felt like not even to be noticed by him in the first place.

I'd also envied Faiza in certain ways, and even told her so, but envy could be such different things. I pitied Gifty for hating rather than loving, and when I thought back to how she would never open up about her past, I knew there must be reasons why she was that way. I might have been the dada ba she saw, clueless about life in her world. But I couldn't be the kind of person who would betray her. I hadn't been sure about that before, because she had betrayed me. But now, talking to Mom, I suddenly was.

"You know, Mom, you should tell Auntie to get a cash till! She wouldn't listen to me, but that drawer she keeps the money in is just not safe."

"You're right, darling. That's exactly why people have cameras in their shops. I'll suggest that to her too."

I smiled. I knew my auntie, and a cash till would be plenty to start with.

After I got ready for bed that night, I read my diary again—all my entries since the day I had arrived at Auntie Lydia's house. I felt like picking up a pen to fill things in—things I understood better now; things left out that I now remembered as I read.

It was a cool night, and my windows were open. I read till the last line and stared out into the night. The scent of jasmine blew in. I nodded slowly. I needed to write this properly—the full, unexpurgated version, pulling together all the different threads from this diary, my article, my memory. I owed it to myself and to Faiza to put down a true record, committing to writing all the little details we'd never want to forget.

This was a story.

I scrambled over to my desk, switched on my lovely new laptop, and opened a fresh document. With the special software, I could lay it out like the pages of a book. I designed the cover, choosing a sky-blue color with an oval inset at the top, in cream. Inside it, I typed in a curly font, bold letters:

The Kaya Girl

It would take many entries to write the story, but I started right then and wrote for hours. I should have been sleepy, but I felt as if I were back in the market with Faiza. It was 4:00 a.m. when my eyelids finally started to droop. I lay in bed, thinking about my beloved friend; wondering where she was now, what she might be doing. Had she made it to Kumasi? Was she busy carrying things in her big bowl for rich customers? Had she found new friends? And, most important, had she found Asana?

Now I knew the pain Faiza must have felt to lose Asana so suddenly, without even the chance for a proper goodbye. And what it must have been like to have no clue where Asana was, how to get back in touch with her, or if she would ever see her again.

How, in this day and age, I wondered for the millionth time, could I have lost touch so utterly and completely with someone who mattered so much?

I imagined looking for Faiza in Kejetia Market— a minute, self-effacing figure in a churning bustle of thousands. I thought, for the hundredth time, of going up north to find her. I couldn't even remember the name of her village, with all those consonants and throaty sounds. All I had left of her were my memories. And her name. Faiza.

What did it mean, anyway? I'd never thought of that when she was right in front of me. But now that it was one of the only things I had left to hold on to, I felt an urgent need to know.

I got out of bed, woke the laptop from sleep, and googled "Faiza." It was worth a try. The directory page loaded. Cool! There were several entries. I clicked.

"*Faiza is a female Arabic name meaning 'winner,' 'successful woman,' 'victorious,'*" I read under my breath.

"Yes!" I said out loud. Faiza might have been a poor

kayayoo, but there was nothing poor about her spirit. She called fear a coward and said it could never stop us if we stopped it first. I had no idea what fate had in store for her, but the meaning of her name only strengthened my faith in her.

"Winner," "victorious," I read again as dawn began to streak the sky.

It seemed almost prophetic.

PART TWO
FIFTEEN YEARS LATER

PART TWO

Chapter 22

WHEN I WOKE UP, THE FIRST THING I SAW WAS MUTED SUNLIGHT through cream curtains. It took my eyes a few moments to adjust. I was in a room. It was cool and quiet and smelled of antiseptic. The only sound was a soft murmur, but I was not sure where it was coming from. There was a flat-screen TV on the wall overhead and a metal stand next to me with a transparent bag that was dripping fluid slowly into a tube curling into a valve attached to the back of my hand.

As I noticed each of these things, I wondered why they, and I, were here. It was bewildering, but I was strangely calm. My head felt quiet and cushioned, as if it were filled with cotton wool and bubbles. Memories began to trickle into my mind. I had been rushed to the hospital. Yes, that was where I was. And...my baby! I didn't quite understand it, but it was the only thing I felt sure about—I must have had...a baby.

I closed my eyes again. Of course—a baby—with Mike! Mike, my old crush from Makola, now my husband. We had bumped into each other again on campus in Legon, at the University of Ghana. My eyes flew wide open. There he was, sitting next to Mom! It was their voices I could hear.

They both rushed over, exclaiming. Mike took my hands in his, trying not to disturb the tubes. Mom stroked my forehead.

"Praise God!" she said, and a tear plopped onto my pillow.

"Mom! What's wrong?"

"Oh, we were just so afraid, darling, for you and the baby. But everything's fine now, and I just—" She put her hands over her face, sat back in her chair, and sobbed.

"It's the relief." Mike put his arm around her. "It's been a tough twenty-four hours for all of us." His hair was unkempt, and he looked exhausted.

Twenty-four hours! How could I have slept that long? "Where's the baby? Where's my baby girl?" I was shouting.

"She's fine!" said Mom. "Don't worry. I told you, everything's fine." She dabbed at her eyes with a handkerchief, still sniffing. Then she stopped. "Wait—how d'you know it's a girl? You said you weren't going to find out."

She was right. I didn't know how I knew.

"Our beautiful little girl is in the incubator room." Mike kissed me on the forehead. "And she's absolutely fine."

I tried to move and felt a sharp pain in my lower abdomen. Memories flooded me now—a dizzy spell, being rushed to Dad's clinic, people milling around me, words floating over my head—*high blood pressure, emergency C-section*—then the operating theater, freezing cold, with bright lights, and masked faces hovering over me.

"Take it easy, sweetheart," said Mom, pushing me gently back against the pillow. "She won't run away, and you needn't worry. She's strong and healthy for a preemie. You're very lucky. And your doctor was wonderful. So calm and capable."

"True." Mike nodded.

"Who was it?"

"None of the ones I know," said Mom. "Must be a new locum. I guess your dad brought in some extra hands for while he's away." She fussed around, tidying up the things on the nightstand by my bed. "Would you like some juice?"

"Water, please," I said. My throat was parched.

Mom poured a glass for me and helped me sit up and drink. Then she took her phone from her bag. "Let me try your Dad again so you can speak to him," she said. "He's been frantic."

"Poor thing," I said. "He was so sure he'd arrive before the baby did."

Mom couldn't get through, so she sent him a message. He was on a lecture tour in the US.

"Auntie Lydia sends love too," said Mike. "She's been calling every few hours."

There was a knock at the door, and a nurse in a white uniform came in. It was time for my blood pressure check.

Mike got up and kissed me again. "We'll be off now, darling."

Mom said she'd return in the evening. She insisted on bringing all my meals. "You're auntie's making you palm soup tomorrow," she called over her shoulder as Mike held the door for her.

"How are you feeling, Mrs. Fosu?" The nurse reached for my hand and checked the valve in the back of it.

"Weak like something."

"We need you to sleep." She reached up to the stand and slowed the speed of the drip. "You gave us such a scare. Doctor stayed with you all night!"

What? It must have been even more serious than I realized. Or maybe because I was the director's daughter. But even then ... "The doctor stayed with me?"

"After your operation. Right here by your side, all through the night."

"Which doctor was that?"

"Dr. Mohammed, madam." She wrapped the blood pressure meter around my upper arm and started to pump it.

"Dr. Mohammed?"

"One of our new doctors."

"I've heard good things about him," I said.

She nodded absently, not really listening as the pump

wheezed in her hand and the wrap tightened around my arm. She stopped and the machine beeped. The wrap hissed as it started to deflate, and I felt the release of pressure. She packed it up.

"Thank you, Mrs. Fosu." She headed for the door. "Doctor will soon be here."

Oh, good. I'd get to meet him.

I lay back on my pillow, too drowsy to stay awake any longer. I thought I heard a knock at the door, and I was dimly conscious of people coming into my room, probably the doctor on his rounds with a nurse. Through the fog I heard voices and felt warm, comforting hands, and then they were gone. I slept through Mom's evening visit, so she left my food with the nurses.

I didn't wake up till the next morning, groggy but better. It was time to see my baby.

"Doctor wants you up today," the nurse said. "We need your blood to circulate so your incision will heal."

The pain was intense, but I made it onto my feet and walked shakily, supported by her. There was only one baby in the incubator room—mine. A young woman in

a white coat and blue surgical cap was standing looking at her. She turned as I entered, and I saw she had
a stethoscope around her neck. The pediatrician, most
likely.

"Mrs. Fosu!" She smiled. "It's good to see you up on
your feet! Your baby is doing very well."

She looked young for a doctor, but she was warm
and had a lovely smile. I was glad she was looking after
my baby.

My baby; my daughter—what wonderful words! She
was tiny but so beautiful, all curled up, asleep. I could
already see a resemblance in the tiny face—the set of the
features—hang on, yes...Auntie Lydia! How delighted
she was going to be! My daughter had a shock of hair in
little, glossy curls, and her minute fingers twitched as
she slept. I longed to touch her.

"You will hold her tomorrow," said the doctor, as if
reading my mind.

"Oh, wonderful!" I clapped my hands.

Mike and Mom were happy to see me so much
stronger that afternoon. They arrived with a huge bunch
of flowers and a heavy food basket from Auntie Lydia
that was covered in a lacy tea towel. The room filled

up with a mixture of scents—sweet flowers and rich, fragrant palm soup.

We went to the incubator room, Mom and Mike supporting me on either side. Our baby opened her eyes briefly and fell asleep again.

"So, what are you going to call my little angel?" Mom asked after they'd helped me back into bed.

"We haven't got that far yet," said Mike. "I'm still taking in the fact that she's here and that Abby's okay." He laid my hand on his cheek.

I had an idea for a name, but I needed to discuss it with him first. We'd thought we had another month to decide. Mom wheeled up the bedside table and ladled soup into a bowl for me. She helped me sit up and eat. The flavors took me right back to Auntie's house, the shop, Makola, times with Faiza.

After they left, the nurse came to give me my injections, and then it was time for the doctor's rounds. This time I was determined to stay awake to meet the famous Dr. Mohammed. He came in with a nurse and unclipped my patient chart from the end of the bed.

"Good afternoon, Doctor!"

He glanced up from the chart. A tall, shy-looking

young man. "Good afternoon, Mrs. Fosu. And how are we feeling today?"

"Much better, thank you."

He inspected my incision, nodding. "Perfect. You are making a great recovery!" He turned to leave.

"Thanks to you, Doctor," I said. "I've been told what good care you took of me."

"You're welcome, Mrs. Fosu, but..." He muttered something to the nurse and turned back to me. "It was actually Dr. Mohammed who performed your operation."

"Oh! I thought you were Dr. Mohammed."

He shook his head. "I'm Dr. Ocran. Dr. Mohammed is in surgery at the moment."

"I beg your pardon," I said. "I didn't realize."

"No problem." He smiled. "Dr. Mohammed should be with you tomorrow."

Chapter 23

THE NEXT MORNING BEGAN ONE OF THE BEST DAYS OF MY LIFE.

When I woke up, the nurse said, "You need to take your bath because a VIP is coming to visit!"

"My baby?"

"Yes!"

She gave me a bed bath, and when it was done, another nurse wheeled in a bassinette with my little girl in it. There were no longer any tubes attached to her. She looked right into my eyes, and I picked her up, marveling. The nurses had selected a peach-and-cream romper with matching booties and crocheted cap for her. A gift from Auntie Lydia, it turned out.

"Congratulations!" they said, and they left us alone.

I pushed my little finger into my daughter's palm and felt her grip it with surprising strength. She was calm, but full of restless baby energy.

"Strong little thing, aren't you?" I stroked her softer-than-soft cheek. I couldn't wait to share her with Mike.

There was a knock at the door. It was the young doctor I'd seen in the incubator room the day before. She smiled, seeing us together. "How is the little lady?"

"Marvelous! I'm so happy."

"That's exactly what we want!"

Her smile reminded me of someone, but I had no idea who. She had the surgical cap on again, so I couldn't see her hair, and in any case, my memory seemed to have gone on holiday after what I'd been through. "Are you here to examine her?"

"No. I'm here to see you. The pediatrician will be along for her later."

She sat in the chair next to my bed, and I caught a glimpse of an African print dress underneath her white coat. She looked so comfortable sitting there that I almost offered her a drink, but that would have been silly.

"I thought *you* were the pediatrician!" I said. Was it me, or was it this clinic? I just couldn't seem to get things straight. Maybe it was all the drugs they'd been giving me.

"Oh no!" She laughed. "I haven't got that far yet. I'm a general practitioner. I'm Dr. Mohammed."

"What? You're Dr. Mohammed?"

"Yes."

"The doctor who saved us two?"

"I'm the doctor who operated on you. I think it was God who saved your lives."

There was something about her cool logic.

"I've been wanting to thank you!"

"You're welcome," she said with a warmth that went right through me. "I'm so glad you're both okay."

I looked at the stethoscope looped over her shoulders, black and silver against the white of her coat. But this was not like talking to a doctor; it was like talking to...a friend.

"Yesterday morning, when I saw you in the incubator room, I'd have thanked you then. But I never thought it was you."

"Why not?"

"Well, for one thing, I thought you were a man!"

"Abba! Is it only men who can be doctors?"

270

What did she say?

I looked at her. She looked coolly back. It couldn't be. It couldn't possibly. Not here, not now, not her. Other people said "abba," even here down south. *Get a grip*, I said to myself, *you're really losing it now*. But, no. It wasn't just the "abba"; it was the whole thing—the way she'd said it, and how it made me feel—foolish yet tickled.

I looked at her cheeks, rounding as a slow smile spread over her face. Two lines, now too faint to be immediately visible, etched vertically in the middle of each cheek. I looked down at my baby, now sleeping softly in my arms, and back up at the smiling face before me.

"Yɛfrɛ me Abena," I said in Twi.

"N yuli Faiza," she said in a language called Dagbanli—I'm Faiza.

A wise person once told me that looking and seeing were not the same thing.

That day, fifteen years later, I found out how right she was. I'd accused other people of making assumptions, and yet I had looked right through Faiza because

I'd never in my wildest dreams imagined she could be a doctor.

I should have known better.

I put my daughter back in the bassinette and fell on her. We shrieked and laughed and cried and laughed some more. Only a newborn baby could have slept through it.

"You bad girl, you knew it was me, but you didn't say anything!"

"I wanted to see how long it would take you to figure it out!"

"No wonder it felt that way chatting to you. I almost offered you a drink!"

"Let's have one now," she said. "I'm off duty." She got up and poured two glasses of fruit juice.

I held out my glass. "To friendship!" We clinked. "Faiza, d'you have any idea how much I've missed you?"

"Yes," she said with that calm I couldn't believe I'd failed to recognize. "Why? You think I didn't miss you?"

"I kept wishing you were here while I was going through all this. Not knowing you were!"

"All the way!" She smiled her oversize smile.

"So, when did you realize it was me?"

"When you called my name."

I felt goose pimples on my arms. "I called your name? When?"

"In the recovery room, after your operation."

I leaned back against my pillow.

"You okay?" she asked.

"Just...trying to get my head around all this!"

She came over to the bed, plumped up my pillows, and tucked the bedclothes in around me. "When I first saw your patient folder with "Roberta Fosu" written on it, I had no idea it was you."

"Yeah, no one calls me Roberta. Just in school and, I guess, here."

She settled herself back on the chair. "During the operation I was too busy to look at your face, but later, when they wheeled you to the recovery room, I came to check if you were coming out of the anesthesia. You were muttering under your breath, like a sleep talker. I was shocked to hear my name. I took a good look at you. And then at this little Lydia here!"

We laughed.

"Faiza, every time something important was happening in my life, it was like you were there."

"I figured something like that when I heard my name come out of your lips. And because I always felt the same way."

"It helped me just thinking of you. Your strength; your name."

"My name?"

"It means 'victorious; successful woman; winner.' I googled it."

She laughed. "I knew it meant something good like that, but I never bothered to google it."

"Well, I think it's a beautiful name, and it's been so precious to me all these years that I couldn't find you. Sometimes I used to say it out loud, just to give myself courage. Maybe that's what I was doing in the recovery room."

"Maybe," she said. "But after I realized it was you, I took your hand and told you that you were going to be okay and that you had a beautiful baby girl."

"So, it *was* you! No wonder it felt so real."

"I wanted to scream and shout and hug you, but you were postoperative and my patient!"

I felt as if we needed years just to tell each other all the things we needed to tell each other. But there was one thing that needed to be said before another word was spoken. The smile faded from my face, and I gazed silently at the flowers by my bedside.

"What is it, Ab?"

"Faiza, I'm sorry. So sorry."

"For what?"

"What happened that day. Please forgive me."

There was silence for a few moments, and Faiza looked at the flowers too. I noticed for the first time how loudly the clock on the wall was ticking.

Then she said, "It's okay, Abena. We both know Gifty cooked up the whole thing."

"Yes, but I didn't stand up for you properly!" I tried to sit up but was stopped short by pain.

"Take it easy there," murmured Faiza.

I supported my incision with my hand and took a deep breath. Emotion was a tougher opponent than pain. "Faiza, I never had to fight for anything in my life like you did. I loved you as a friend and a sister, but I couldn't defend you when Auntie accused you. Or stop her from sending you away. All because you were a kayayoo."

"But it was hard for you because you had disobeyed her."

"That was what I told myself for ages, but it was just an excuse. What kind of rules were they, anyway? Auntie would never have barred my school friends from her shop. She'd never have dreamed of accusing them like that! And if she had, I'd have told my parents and made her take it back. But with you, I was afraid. I couldn't admit it to myself, but I feared humiliation, rejection, for standing up for a kayayoo."

"You're wrong that you never had to fight, Abena," said Faiza. "Every day of our friendship was a battle for you—against other people. If you hadn't fought it, we could never have been friends in the first place. You might have been afraid, but you're a lot stronger than you know, my friend."

"But, Faiza"—I was crying now—"I let you down when it mattered most."

"Oh, Abena!" She sat on the bed and put her arm around me. "To defend me that day, you'd have had to stand up not only to your aunt but to a whole mindset, a whole way of thinking. That battle isn't only yours to fight. You were just a kid, brave enough to step out of her cozy world and open her heart to the unknown. If that's not courage, I don't know what is. There's nothing to forgive, silly girl, because I never held it against you."

She hugged me, and relief flooded me, at last.

"You're so strong, Faiza," I said over her shoulder.

She listened for what would come next.

"And I'm a stronger person for knowing you."

She nodded her approval at this amendment.

"And I for knowing you. D'you know, Ab, that you are the best teacher I ever had? That first science lesson you gave me—you have no idea what it led to!"

"Tell me."

"You want to hear my story?"

I nodded.

She propped me up on my pillows again and sat back on the chair by my bedside.

Chapter 24

"That last day you saw me," she began, "was the day I left for Kumasi."

"I know."

"How?"

"Because I looked everywhere for you, and you were just gone—in a way you'd never been before."

"I thought you might. But...it was time to move on."

"I know."

"I took the night bus straight to Kumasi and arrived the next morning. Wow, Kejetia was as big as we'd said. I started work that same day. I was exhausted, but I had to...occupy my mind."

"Yeah."

"And I needed to meet other kayayei to start asking about Asana. They knew the name—you see, where we come from, it's a name for any girl twin, so there were many around, from villages all over the North. I must have met all the Asanas in Kejetia except the one I was looking for.

"After a month, I was ready to give up. One Saturday morning, I bought a beautiful set of English bowls for Auntie Fati and sweets for the children. I was going to catch the night bus to Tamale.

"That afternoon, a customer called me into a seamstress's shop. She was picking up some clothes and needed help with her shopping. One of the seamstress's apprentices packed the new clothes into a plastic bag. A quiet young lady, smart in her gray-and-green uniform. As she handed it to me, our eyes met. I gasped.

" 'Ɛyɛ dɛn?' she asked in Twi. 'What is it?'

" 'Kayayoo, ka wo ho! Hurry up!' My customer was already standing outside the shop.

" 'Wait!' the girl said as I turned to follow.

"But I couldn't lose my customer, or I might be accused of stealing her goods.

" 'I'll be back.' I rushed off.

"Asana! It had to be. But then why didn't she know me? And what was she doing here, in a seamstress's shop, of all places? As soon as I'd seen my customer off, I ran back to the shop, but she was gone! I asked one of the other apprentices for her.

" 'She asked permission to go on break,' she said. 'I think she went to look for you.'

"Oh God. How would I find her now? I could wait at the shop, but once she got back, her madam wouldn't want her chatting to people. I had to find her while she was still free.

"I walked up and down, looking around me at every step. People must have been wondering why I kept turning my head as if I were watching a football match. I saw pig feet and cow tails, salted and smoked fish, herbs and spices, powders and pastes, clothes and shoes, bags and belts, tall people, short people, fat people, thin people, selling, buying, eating, sleeping, playing, fighting, chatting, laughing . . . but none of them were her.

"Tears came into my eyes. I felt so defeated. Then someone bumped hard into me from behind, and I swung round.

" 'Asana!'

" 'Faiza!'

"We had bumped straight into each other, back-to-back. We jumped into each other's arms, both crying, both laughing. It was like with you just now—we were so happy, we didn't know what to do. We must have been making so much noise, but in the chaos of Kejetia, it was like we were in our own private world. We sat down, I don't even remember what on, and told each other as much as we could in the few minutes she had left. I asked why she hadn't recognized me.

" 'Because I never expected to see you here, Faiza!' she said. 'It was like I was looking straight at you and just not seeing you!' "

"You were so right about that, Faiza," I cut in. "About looking without seeing."

"But I was doing it myself, just assuming Asana would be a kayayoo! I never expected, never even thought of looking for her in a seamstress's shop. But she'd been lucky. She had carried the seamstress's machine for her one day after closing, and the woman had found her respectful and started using her regularly.

She liked Asana so much that she asked if she would like to become an apprentice. Asana was only too happy to stop being a kayayoo and learn a skill.

"I told her I'd looked for her in Accra, and she said she and the girls she'd run away with had found out at the lorry station that morning that fuel prices had gone up the day before. Most of them couldn't afford the fare to Accra, so they had to stop in Kumasi. She couldn't believe I'd gone all that way to find her, but I told her I'd been fine and even found a new friend in Accra. She was so happy to hear that, and she was dying for news from home. I said everyone was fine when I left, and that her mother missed her and was looking forward to seeing her again.

" 'But I'm not going back!' she cried. 'No way!'

" 'Asana, you don't have to worry about Alhaji Brown Teeth anymore.'

" 'Yes, but who will it be next? There's nothing my mother can do if my father decides to marry me off again.'

"I could not argue with that. And I agreed it would be foolish to give up her apprenticeship.

" 'I will go home one day, Faiza, but... only when I'm ready.'

"I hugged her and said I'd do the same in her shoes."

"I didn't leave for Tamale that night after all, and we spent the whole of Sunday together, catching each other up on the details we hadn't had time for the day before.

" 'Faiza, you know what?' said Asana. 'Why don't you just stay here? I'll convince Madam to take you on as an apprentice. Imagine, learning and working together side by side!'

"It was so tempting, but I told Asana I couldn't fail in my promise to Auntie Fati. Asana was worried that her father would try to marry me off too if I went back. I said I could look after myself.

" 'As for that, Faiza, I don't doubt it!' She laughed, but I could see she was still worried.

"We spent the following Sunday together too. I was putting off thinking about leaving, but she brought it up herself.

" 'Faiza, I've been thinking. Magical as it is to be together again, your time is too precious to waste as a kayayoo. You're too smart for that. If you won't stay and work here, then go and do something better back home.'

"I looked at her. She had really changed since those days when she lay helpless on the mat.

"'Faiza, build yourself up so no one can ever force you into anything again. Tell my mother it is my wish that you learn a trade. I'll give you some money toward your own apprenticeship.'

"I started to protest, but she held up a hand. 'Please, my sister, it's the least I can do after what you have done for me.'

"'As you wish.'

"She smiled. 'Maybe one day you and I will start a business together! It's you who taught me, Faiza—we can do wonders if we just believe in ourselves.'"

"I left for Tamale the very next day with the money tied securely inside my wrapper cloth.

"Asana had given me some for her mother too.

"My arrival caused a great stir. I was told that Auntie Fati ran all the way home from her farm when she heard I was back! She hugged me, panting, and thanked God for my safe arrival. Then she asked about Asana.

" 'I have news of her, Auntie!'

"She covered her face with her hands. I put my arm around her and led her to her room. 'Let's talk inside.'

"I settled her on the bed and myself on a stool, savoring the sights and smells of home: the dim coolness of the room, my old friends—the towering stacks of pots and pans, the smokiness from the hearth outside, and the unbeatable aroma of home-cooked food.

"Auntie Fati wept tears of joy and sorrow that day, in which order I'm not sure even she knew. Hearing that her daughter was alive and well, fending for herself and learning a trade, was a joy Auntie could barely contain. But the tears came fast when she realized Asana was not coming back.

"She dried them when I gave her the money Asana had sent. Then I told her about Asana's request for me.

" 'Faiza, my daughter,' she said, 'you have done so much for me. I've missed you, but I have learned to manage without you. You have my blessing to do as Asana wishes.'

"I started making inquiries the very next day about apprenticeships. There was nothing like that in our village, so I went to the next one, which was larger. That was when I found out there was some new program in that community, giving free afternoon classes for children who had never been to school, teaching them to read and write in Dagbanli! It was like a dream come true. I told Auntie Fati that that was what I wanted to do. It suited her even better because I could still help in the house, and I didn't even need to spend any money because there were no uniforms, and everything was free.

"Because of what I'd already learned from Asana and from you, I picked up the reading very fast. I was able to transfer to junior high school in less than a year. That was when I used my savings and the money Asana had given me to buy uniforms and books. The English I'd learned in Accra helped me so much in school, and all the other things you'd taught me too. Abena, within five years of leaving Makola, I got the highest BECE results in the district!"

"What? *What?*"

"Yes! I was called to the District Education Office for an awards ceremony for the best-performing junior high graduates. They announced that the District Chief

Executive was giving me a scholarship to senior high as a motivation to all the children in the district. Our district had been doing badly, you see, and so many girls were leaving to become kayayei in the cities."

"Oh, Faiza! Victorious Faiza! I knew you could do it!"

"Thanks to you, Abena!" She smiled. "I'll never forget the day you revealed the world to me."

"And I'll never forget the orange and the lime." I laughed. "And the market women!"

"See, that's what I meant when I said you were my best teacher. After you made it all fall into place like that, I had to know everything else that was out there."

"So, what happened next?"

"I went to Tamale Girls for senior high school. That was when I left home for the second time, for the boarding house in Tamale. Auntie Fati was crying and laughing at the same time! My uncle didn't see what a girl needed all that education for, but she told him nobody was asking him to pay and she could manage without me. And you know what else happened then? Asana came home!"

"Yay! At last."

"But only for a visit. She brought enough money for her father to see it was better to leave her in peace than to try and force her into marriage. I don't think he'd have dared try, anyway, because she was a whole new person. Auntie was ecstatic. She wanted her to stay, but Asana said she needed to start her own business. She had good contacts and a good clientele in Kejetia. She recruited some apprentices from the village to take back to Kumasi with her."

"What about Malik?"

Faiza was amazed I still remembered his name.

"And his dimples," I said. "I still remember those dimples!"

"He was right there in the village!" she said, "along with the dimples! But he hadn't been able to further his education because his family couldn't afford it. He'd done well as a farmer, though."

"So, was there still any chance for the two of them?"

"He was already married with children, so Asana would have had to be a second wife. She wasn't interested. And he couldn't have coped with the woman she'd become." Faiza smiled. "But anyway, the real point is, she was dating a young man in Kumasi. Also a Dagomba working down south."

"Cool!" I recovered quickly from the loss of the dimples.

"Asana was still with us when the time came for me to leave for senior high. She escorted me to Tamale and gave me money again. She told me never to stop following my dreams, and we said goodbye once again. But the goodbyes were getting easier because each time I was surer about seeing her again. I wished her luck with her young man, and she smiled. 'I will keep you posted!' she said—in English!"

"So, how was senior high school?"

"Hard work and very strict."

I chuckled. "Remember when all you used to go on about was school?"

"Oh, but I was excited to be there, and I enjoyed my studies. One lady from the afternoon classes program back in the village, Auntie Adiza—she used to visit me at school and inspect my reports. She had so much faith in me that she helped me apply for university scholarships in my final year. I passed my SSCE with the best aggregate and got a scholarship to study medicine in America!"

It was like my father's story all over again, but even better.

"Oh, Faiza! I used to think about you all the time, where you were, what you were doing, but I never dared hope you'd get this far!"

"Nor did I! And everything always seemed to happen so fast."

"So, when did you get back from the US?"

"Last year. I could have specialized, but I wanted to come home first and learn more about our medical problems here. Where I come from, they're still so short of doctors and medical facilities."

"That's what Dad said."

"Oh yes—your dad!" She smiled. "Such a legend in tropical diseases. That's why I took the locum here. Only to find out he's none other than your dad!"

"And you know what? He's worked in the North before!"

"So I've heard. I can't wait to meet him!"

"Oh! You haven't yet?"

"No. My main job is at the Korle Bu hospital. I only started here a couple of weeks ago. Dr. Ampiah set it up, and he said your dad had approved it, but we weren't actually able to meet before he left. I don't usually spend this much time here, but I took time off from Korle Bu because of you."

"Did you really sit with me all night after my operation?"

"Abba!" she said. "Pa mabihi n nyɛ ti? Are you not my sister? Would you not do the same for me?"

What would I not do for this unbelievable girl, now that I'd got her back?

Chapter 25

"FAIZA," I WROTE ON THE FLYLEAF OF THE BABY BOOK DAD HAD brought me. And below, in brackets, "Victorious. Successful woman. Winner."

It was the only name for a baby girl who had been delivered by such a woman.

Mike was happy with it. "You don't have to be Muslim to have an Arabic name," he said. I'd finally told him Faiza's story.

"You mean to tell me that that stylish young lady at the market with you that day was a kayayoo?" he asked. "Wait till Steve hears this!"

"Don't you dare tell him!"

"Why does it matter now?"

"It's just . . . for her to decide what matters, that's all."

"My lips are sealed. But if she's going to, then tonight's the night."

It was a month later, and Dad was throwing a party to celebrate the baby, my recovery, and my reunion with Faiza. It was a warm evening at the end of May, and the terrace had been lit with lanterns and decorated with flowers. There were floating candles in the pond and fairy lights in the trees. When Faiza arrived, a hush fell, and everyone turned toward her and clapped.

She put her hands up to her cheeks as she stepped onto the terrace and gave that smile that lit up her entire surroundings. She was wearing a fitted white top with a flowing skirt in a blue-and-white African print, with a small headpiece tied the way her scarf in the market used to be and braids going down her back. She was still tiny but with a lovely figure now, and her heels made her taller. She had always had a way of making simplicity striking, I thought as she walked toward us.

One by one, people went up to her and hugged her. Mom and Mike first, then Auntie Lydia. Auntie held out both hands and Faiza took them.

"Oh, Faiza," she said, "I am so—"

"It's okay, Auntie Lydia," Faiza cut in gently. "You don't have to say anything."

"Then please come back to the shop for a visit," said Auntie. "I'd be honored."

"I'd love to." Faiza glanced at me. "We'll come together."

Next, I got to introduce Faiza to Dad—at last.

"So, this is the famous kayayoo doctor!" He hugged her first, and then they shook hands. "Dr. Mohammed; Faiza the great! You are welcome! We owe you a great deal. It's a pleasure to meet you and an honor to have you at my clinic. Enjoy the party, and see you at work on Monday."

I led her down into the garden to meet the rest of Mike's family. Even Uncle Yaw was there—Mr. Blankson himself, beaming at everyone. But the last person needed no introduction.

"Finally!" Steve said as they shook hands.

Phew! I said in my head.

"I hear you've been asking about me," said Faiza serenely.

"Only for the past fifteen years." He shrugged. "No big deal. Except for that ice cream you still owe me!"

Faiza looked at me.

I grimaced. "Yeah, I meant to tell you...."

Steve stared at me.

"But he can tell you himself now! There's all the time in the world. And lots of ice cream!" I beat a hasty retreat.

I went inside and up to my old bedroom. Little Faiza was just stirring in her Moses basket. She looked at me, bright eyes wide open, so I took her downstairs to join the party. Faiza and Steve were still chatting by the pond when I stepped onto the terrace.

Auntie Lydia rushed over. "Give me my daughter o!" She took the baby out of my arms and cooed at her. "They gave you her name, but your face is mine!" She pointed comically to her own face, bringing on one of little Faiza's dazzling new smiles.

Faiza strolled over with Steve. "*Woi!*" she said. "*Faiza bila!*"

"What does that mean?" Steve asked.

"Faiza Junior," I said.

"Ha, you still remember your Dagbanli!" Faiza smiled.

"You'll have to teach me some," Steve said to her.

She turned back to her namesake. "Bo ka a diri kati nabi lala?"

"Lost me there!" I grinned.

"I asked if someone is paying her to grow."

Baby Faiza kicked up her legs, and for the first time, I heard something from her that sounded like a giggle. My most enduring image of that evening is of my two Faizas, one in the other's arms, wreathed in smiles.

❀

A week later, Faiza and I were at Auntie Lydia's shop. It was a windy day with the sun and clouds playing hide-and-seek in the transition between seasons.

So much had changed in fifteen years, but the shop and its surroundings were still a trove of memories for us. It was bigger now, with a greater variety of goods, and there were mirrors everywhere, which made it look huge. Auntie had a computerized cash till now, and a couple of uniformed assistants who politely offered us refreshments. She'd also introduced a new section for bridal fabrics and accessories, with poster-size photos of bridal me all over, effervescent in tulle, lace, and seed pearls.

"*Mbo!*" Faiza gasped. "My sister is so beautiful."

"She was the most beautiful bride I've ever seen," said Auntie. "And I've seen a lot."

I rolled my eyes and Faiza grinned. We went from shelf to shelf, oohing and aahing at laces, velvets, silks, and satins in shades that defied description, some changing color depending which side you cocked your head. These days it wasn't only Dubai; Auntie shopped in India, China, Indonesia, Switzerland. "You're not a market queen anymore," I said to her. "You're a market empress!"

"You'd better believe it!"

She had mannequins all over the shop that actually looked like African women—and men—dressed like queens and kings in creations tailored from print and lace, topped with embroidered caps and towering geles that were pinned with glittering brooches and strung with beads and pearls. Two queenly specimens stood turned inward, as if admiring each other's fine feathers. Faiza winked at me.

"Auntie," I called over to her at the desk. "You'll have to name these two divas after us!"

"Done!"

We browsed the heritage section, still my favorite. There was mud cloth from Mali, aso oke from Nigeria, kente from Ghana, and . . . Faiza pounced on a blue-and-white cloth. "Mbo! Just like Auntie Fati's!"

It was a handwoven cloth from the North. There was a whole selection of them.

Auntie Lydia smiled. "I have a new fuugu supplier from Daboya! He said they dye their own threads up there, with indigo."

My eye was caught by a shimmering blend of kente and aso oke. "It's called kente oke," Auntie said. I unfolded a piece in shades of orange and rust and sighed, holding it against myself in the mirror.

"It's yours!" Auntie watched, smiling. "Today is a special day. Lydia's Palace and Makola Market welcome you back. You cannot leave empty-handed."

She came and took out a heavy package from the glass cabinet, wrapped in gold paper and tied with white ribbons. "This one is for you, Faiza!"

Faiza put her hands up to her face. I could see it was

the last thing she'd expected. Auntie had known she'd be too modest to choose anything for herself.

"Go on," I said. "Open it!"

There were three cloths in Faiza's package. A matching pair at the top was a ladies' set of fuugu in a striped weave—wavy white interspersed with wider bands of blue in different shades.

"I chose this cloth for you because of its name, Faiza," Auntie said. "I asked my supplier to write it down."

"Northern cloths have names too?" I asked.

"Beautiful ones!" said Auntie. "For beautiful cloths."

Auntie Lydia praising the North! Now I'd seen everything.

She took out a card from a fold of the cloth and handed it to Faiza.

" 'Alieŋdeŋi,' " read Faiza carefully.

"What language is that?" I asked.

"If it's from Daboya then it must be Gonja." Slowly, she read the translation: " 'If people tell lies about you, God will clear your name.' "

I had never seen Faiza cry before, not even on that unspeakable day fifteen years ago. Now I did, and Auntie too. "Faiza, you've been an education for one silly old market queen," she said, sniffing.

I had to come to their rescue. And my own. "Let's see this other one." I pointed at the last cloth, a sparkly lace.

It flashed a million specks as Faiza and I opened it out, flooding me with memories, though it was not peach but a delicate champagne color. A cloth fit for an engagement ceremony, a princess, a queen; it must have been the most exquisite lace in the shop. I thought back to a time when I'd wondered if a poor kayayoo would ever own rich cloth.

We didn't even want to fold it up again. We just stood there, holding it up between us as if we'd captured a ray of moonlight embedded with twinkling stars. It was that hidden brilliance that I loved, revealed in all its glory. My auntie had found the perfect cloths for Faiza. She had said sorry in style.

"I don't know how—" Faiza began, but Auntie held up a warning finger.

"Don't say a word!"

Faiza dropped her end of the cloth, rushed over, and hugged her.

Gathering up the sparkling folds, I knew all pain between the three of us had been laid to rest for good.

When I finished folding it up, I said, "Auntie Lydia, w'ayɛ adeɛ—you have done well! But, as everybody knows"—and she chorused with me—"*every good lace needs a good gele!*"

"Don't worry," she said. "Auntie Omo is expecting you!"

We went next door, where there were more hugs and exclamations—"*Ah-ah!* Look at you two, all grown up!"

Auntie Omotola fussed over us like a mother hen that had finally discovered her lost chicks. She took our new cloths from us to select the best matches from her rainbow assortment of geles.

"Kente oke!" She studied mine, chuckling. "Ghana and Nigeria in perfect harmony!"

"Na wa o!" said Auntie.

Auntie Omo selected a rich burgundy gele with faint lines of gold, which did not at first seem like the best color match to me. She took out her newspaper and pins. With her magic fingers, she folded and tucked and pulled and pushed and twisted and turned, and the tiny pins vanished completely into the frills and flares of the masterpiece.

She pushed me in front of the mirror, opened out the larger piece of my kente-oke set, and tied it around my hips. She slung it coquettishly lower on the right side and arced the folds beautifully into a knot on my left hip. She draped the smaller piece over my left shoulder, all the way down to my wrist. Then she set the pièce de résistance carefully on my head.

Faiza clapped, and I swiveled like a peacock in front of the mirror, marveling at myself and at Auntie Omo, who had known from the beginning that the burgundy headdress would pick out the same shade, hidden between the bolder motifs of my cloth.

It was Faiza's turn.

Auntie Omo opened out her lace with a low whistle. "My daughter," she said in her singsong accent, "your auntie is really welcoming you back."

I was still preening in front of the mirror, so I hardly noticed as Auntie Omo started to fold Faiza's gele. When I finally started paying attention, it was almost done. The color was as delicate as that of her cloth—a cream with a translucent gold sheen that was visible from certain angles but not from others. Her lace was in one piece, so Auntie Omo folded and draped it around her, passing it under one shoulder and over the other, toga-style, and pinning it at the back to fit the waist. Then she lowered the gele onto her head.

Faiza and I looked at each other in the mirror, transported back in time to the one secret we had kept. But this time we didn't need to hide our finery or give it back. And it was no surprise that Faiza looked like a queen of African legend. I'd known she would. The older ladies were tongue-tied. Auntie Lydia finally broke the silence.

"They're even more beautiful than I expected."

"*Chai!*" said Auntie Omo. "This is just too good. Now we have to find something to dress them for!"

I knew what was coming.

"Faiza, you get some young man, abi?"

Auntie Lydia looked on, all ears, hoping for another bride to busy herself with.

Faiza had told me she'd nearly got engaged to an American back in the US. "But in the end, it wasn't fair to him," she'd said. "I needed someone who was part of my own world, because this is where I want to be."

I knew someone else who'd love to see her like this. But I said, "Abeg o! Stop the old lady kokonsa and leave my sister alone!"

They giggled like the old gossips they were.

We thanked Auntie Omo and headed back to Lydia's Palace. As Auntie opened the door, I stopped Faiza and held her back. Auntie looked over her shoulder and smiled, closing the door behind her.

Chapter 26

I DUSTED OFF THE LITTLE STEP OUTSIDE THE SHOP AND SAT DOWN gingerly in my kente oke, feeling the chilled air from under the door seep icily into the small of my back. Faiza hitched up her lace toga, and we both thought of her old silver bowl. She had traded it in for much smaller ones full of syringes and cotton wool.

At that very moment the door opened, and Auntie handed out a small stool. We laughed as Faiza settled herself opposite me. Passersby must have wondered why such a pair of elegant ladies were perched outside a shop like market urchins, but we didn't care. We were carefree girls once again.

Faiza's phone rang, and she took it out of her bag. I saw the caller's name—Steve.

She let it ring.

"Go on, answer it."

"Not now."

"When you're alone, right?"

"Not that..."

I arched an eyebrow.

"Well, not only that..." She smiled. "It's just that there's a time for everything, Abena. These past fifteen years, you have no idea how many times I've wished I was right here with you. Today has been a gift, and right now is our time."

I smiled. It was the perfect moment. "Faiza, would you like to hear my story?"

She stared and then smiled, nodding.

I hitched the shimmering orange fabric over my arm and pulled out a sky-blue book from my handbag, opened it, and started reading. The wind picked up around us, and beyond the shop, dust swirled up gently into the air.

"*Mbo!*" she said after the first paragraph. "You wrote about me?"

"About us." I smiled.

"Let me see!"

I handed her the bound printout of my manuscript.

"'The Kaya Girl,'" she read, a smile encircling her face. "That would be...me?"

I nodded, remembering how my teacher had rolled the r in "girl" and thinking how you wouldn't know from Faiza's accent that she'd ever been to the US, let alone lived there for seven years.

"More! Read more!" She handed it back to me, so excited she could hardly sit still.

Storm clouds subdued the sun's glare as I read, and Faiza's lace and gele took on different sheens. We should probably have been worrying about getting rained on in all our finery, but we were elsewhere altogether, back in the world of our childhood. I finished the first chapter and looked up at her.

She sat as if in a trance. "Go on!"

It would have taken all day to read the whole thing, so I skipped bits here and there so that I could catch her up with my life since our time together in the market. She couldn't wait to hear how Mike and I had found each other again. "D'you remember how you sneaked that photo of him?" she asked. "That crappy one you showed me the first time we talked...or rather, sang? At the plantain seller's?"

There were no words for what it felt like to laugh together over things I'd ached for years to tell her about. Half reading, half filling in the details, I shared with her how, at the end of my first semester at the University of Ghana, I'd seen a flyer pinned to my hall's notice board for Shakespeare's *Romeo and Juliet* at the amphitheater in Commonwealth Hall. As I sat in the front row, munching plantain chips and popcorn with my friends, Romeo had seemed familiar to me. He got the loudest cheers from the audience, especially when he met Juliet and gave her a dazzling smile—the Grin, white against black. I knew at that moment who he was.

I wasn't sure he'd remember me, but at the end of the play, I left my friends and my date, Theo, to go over and say hi. As I climbed over the stone benches, I saw another girl go up and link her arm through his. She reminded me of the film star Jackie Appiah. I turned away, but Mike called out through the sea of faces. "Abena!"

He couldn't possibly mean me, I told myself. Abena

was an Akan name for girls born on a Tuesday. There could be any number of us here. But still, there was something about the way he said it that made me feel like the only Abena in the world. I turned around. He was staring directly at me. I walked unsteadily to the stage.

"Abena!" He held out his hand. "What are you doing here?"

"A BA in English." I knew he'd be surprised I hadn't gone abroad for university, but Dad had insisted. He'd said that it was time for me to get into the Ghanaian system and that I could always go abroad for a master's degree.

"Okay!" said Mike. *And how is the dada bee managing here in Legon?* his smile asked, still as eloquent as ever.

"And you?" I asked.

"Electrical engineering. Final year."

"Right. And where's your brother?" I kicked myself as the words came out.

"Steve? In Kumasi—Tech. And your friend?"

"Actually," I said, "she was heading to Kumasi too, last time I saw her."

"Well, well," he said. "Maybe he'll find her at last, eh?"

"Mikey, we need to get going," his girlfriend purred.

"Oh, sorry," he said. "Abena, this is Isabella. Izzy, this is Abena, an old friend."

As she pulled him away, he said over his shoulder, "You still owe me an ice cream, you know!"

"So do you!" I called back.

"So you know Romeo!" said Theo, coming up behind me. "Who is he?"

I looked into the play program and read out, " 'Michael Fosu.' "

Faiza chuckled. "And may I ask how long Mike and Izzy lasted after that?"

"Not long." I grinned.

"You and your Mike! From Makola to the altar!"

"I wasn't going to let him slip through my fingers again, was I? And the wedding was beautiful. You missed, pah! Auntie Lydia pulled out all the stops—you've seen the photos."

"This your auntie!"

"Yeah, we've come a long way. I didn't see her for years after we left the market, you know. But in the end she couldn't blind herself anymore. Gifty got too bold. Started smuggling fabrics out of the shop to sell for herself."

"Wow! So, what happened?"

"Auntie sent her back to her people in the village. She even told me one day that she was sorry about what had happened with you all those years ago."

Faiza smiled. "She reminds me of Auntie Fati."

"They're two of a kind, from the sounds of it! Anyway, when Mike and I got engaged, Auntie went all the way to Dubai to buy fabrics and stuff for the engagement ceremony and the whole wedding party. Took us to her top designer. Come and see her, fussing around with the bridesmaids and flower girls! On the day, she came to dress me together with Mom. She tried to hide it, but I saw tears in her eyes when she pulled the veil over my face."

I could see from Faiza's face that she was thinking of her own auntie again.

"I chose her to help us cut the cake. You should have seen her; as if she had been elected president of Ghana! Then Mike and I opened the floor. Guess the song we chose?"

"*No one be like you,*" Faiza sang.

"Mike sang it out loud to me and got the rest of the guests to join in! And his gift to me was this huge, hi-tech TV. He said it was fully compatible with everything."

"Mike, pah!" Faiza laughed.

"Oh, we had so much fun that day. The only thing missing was you. My roommate from Legon was maid of honor, and she did a great job, but... it wasn't the same."

"Oh, Ab, I'd have given anything to be there!"

"Steve missed you too. He was best man. When I mentioned you at rehearsals, he told me to look for you on social media! I bet he did a search himself!"

"Stubborn guy!" She smiled.

"You were there in spirit, though, at least for me. And we'll make up for it, at your wedding!"

"Don't get carried away now!" She pointed at the book. "There's more to read, isn't there?"

"Oh yes, lot's more, but it's not complete yet."

"Why not?"

"Well, I've had a lot of catching up to do now that I've found you again!"

"So, once you add the new stuff, it'll be done, right?"

"Not really."

She frowned. "Why not?"

"I'm not quite sure how to end it, you see. It's kind of...not over yet. I mean, here we are now, and—what happens next?"

"Oh yes, I see what you mean!" She thought for a moment. "I suppose we're just going to have to live it!"

"Exactly! But maybe it will help if we guess...or imagine some of it in advance."

"Yes! After all, we both have dreams, don't we?"

"What are yours, Faiz?"

"Oh, Ab, there's so much I want to do, I don't even know where to start!"

I chuckled.

"What are you laughing at?"

"The last time you said that to me, I offered to teach you to read. Remember? And now look at you—from porter to doctor!"

She smiled. "And now I want to specialize."

"Of course. In what?"

"Public health, I think. That's what's really needed where I come from, and I'd like to go back and work there, at least for some time."

"That'd be so great!"

A gust of wind frisked around us, ruffling the awning over the shop front. Passersby picked up speed and the market stirred to the bluff of the clouds. I felt a stray drop on my arm. "Shall we go in?"

She shook her head. "This one will pass."

"How can you be so sure?"

"Have you forgotten how I used to walk around this market all day?"

We laughed. "Hey, d'you think the open-air restaurant is still there?"

"Good question," she said. "I'm getting hungry. Let's go see!"

"Dressed like this?" Then I laughed at my own question, and we said, at the same time, "*Yes!*"

I pointed at the sky. "But let's give this a couple more minutes to clear up. So, have you been home since you got back from the States?"

"Oh, loads. I went as soon as I got back."

"What was it like to see everyone again?"

"Amazing! Auntie Fati ran all the way from her farm again! A bit slower this time, though. They've all aged, and she's been suffering from arthritis. In fact, I'll be going again soon, to take her some medication."

"Can I come?"

"As soon as little Faiza is old enough for you to travel, I'd like nothing more, Ab!"

I pictured what it would be like to see, at last, all the things she'd talked about, meet all the people I'd got to know through her stories.

"So, what about Asana?"

"Asana's back home now! Well, not exactly, but close by. She owns the biggest tailoring shop in Tolon, and we've gone into business together! She'll soon be opening a boutique in Tamale."

"*Awesome!*"

"As a matter of fact, I need to ask Auntie Lydia for some business advice for her."

"Auntie will be so psyched to help. You know what—how about you invite Asana down for a visit to see Lydia's Palace for herself? I'll set it up with Auntie!"

"Brilliant!"

"I can't wait to meet her. So, did she get married in the end?"

"Yeah! To that guy I told you about. He's working in Tamale. They have three children now."

"Good for her!"

"Auntie Fati keeps telling me to follow in her footsteps. She's so proud of me, but you know our people—having children is always more important to them than anything else a woman could possibly do."

At least no one could ever force Faiza to marry anyone now, I thought, regardless of the color of his teeth. "So, are you going to oblige them?" I grinned.

"One day, I guess, but not just yet. I have so much to do first, Abena."

"So you do," I said gravely. "For a start, you'd better get serious about collecting those English bowls, my girl!"

"And you say I'm the cheeky one!"

"Just don't leave it too late, Faiz, okay?"

"I'll do my best."

The sun was out again, the clouds receding, wind subsiding. I reached for Faiza's hand and squeezed it. "You this kaya girl, you have no idea how proud I am of you!"

"Aw, thanks, Ab. But I hope you don't envy me anymore!"

"Well, there's just this teeny little thing...."

She rolled her eyes. "Tell me."

"It's been amazing becoming a mother, but when I look at you, I wish I could be as professional, as independent."

"It's not easy balancing everything, Ab, and I'm so proud of you too. But I know there's still a globe-trotting journalist in there."

I laughed.

"Hey, whatever happened with that competition— that article you were doing on the market. Remember?"

"Funny you should ask!" I took a brown envelope out of my bag and handed it to her.

"Mbo!" She pulled out a printout. "*Published!* Second place in the Urban Bustle category! What did I tell you? Seriously, Ab, you should go back to school as soon as you can and do your master's. You have to chase those dreams!"

"That's exactly what I've been thinking. You see, our story kept me writing all this time and...I guess that's what I still want to do with my life."

"You've always been amazing at it, Abee. You'll make a totally awesome journalist."

"How can you be so sure?"

"Abba! You don't have to be called Faiza to be a winner!"

It seemed so simple when she said it like that. Her faith in me was so unquestioning that I felt silly for doubting myself; I felt like I could actually start planning toward it.

"And I'll keep writing our story," I said.

"Well then, we've got some living to do!"

She rose from her stool, curtsied with an extravagant flourish, and held out her hand to me. I took it and minced down the step with my nose in the air.

We set off into the market in our finery, laughing out loud, the freedom of it filling us up with lightness as our laughter blended into the chaotic swirl of the market and rose above it, lifting our souls up into the sky, free as the birds.

A Word on Language

IF YOU WERE TO TRAVEL TO GHANA, AND ESPECIALLY IF YOU SPENT time in Makola Market like Abena and Faiza, you would hear a vast array of languages around you. Language is a living, constantly evolving thing, and the linguistic diversity of Ghana reflects our rich cultural heritage. While English is Ghana's official language due to its colonial history, there are over fifty indigenous languages still in everyday use. In addition, we have blends of European and indigenous languages, known as pidgins, as well as African languages and pidgins from neighboring countries, especially Nigeria, that have mingled with our own.

In writing *The Kaya Girl*, conveying a flavor of our indigenous languages and pidgins was an important part of setting the scene. I know most readers will not be familiar with all the different languages used, so I did my best to ensure that the context around words written in languages other than English expressed their meaning.

I am hoping that, like Abena and Faiza when they first meet, readers will discover that understanding is not always dependent on speaking the same language. I encourage readers who would like to learn more to do their own research into specific words or aspects of Ghanaian culture.

Acknowledgments

I THANK MY AGENT, CHARLOTTE SHEEDY, AND MY EDITOR, SUSAN Rich, for loving this story enough to bring it to an international audience and for being so incredibly supportive, outstanding, and fun to work with. Susan's creative vision and professional expertise have enriched not only the story but my life as a writer. My thanks also to Ally Sheedy for her early editorial work.

Many friends and fellow writers have played diverse roles in this story's journey, and I am grateful to them all, including Catherine McKinley for two decades of writing mentorship, Elizabeth-Irene Baitie for first encouraging me to try my hand at writing for children, Louise Lynas and Toyin Dania for critical early feedback, and Ato Quayson for moral support during the process of first publication. I also thank Kinna Likimani and Todd Moss for helpful advice about publication.

For their love, laughter, unflagging support, and faith in me, I thank Erin Haney, Afia Atta-Agyemang, Nana Darkoa Sekyiamah, Tina Heinel-Kassardjian, Karine and Liam McVeigh, Inken Bruns, Angela Vanderpuije, Rebecca Awuah, Dörthe Wacker, Donna Sheppard, and Brooks Anne Robinson.

A big thank-you to Katie Abu for bringing about my first work adventure in northern Ghana, and to all who warmly welcomed me over years of research and helped me get to know, love, and be inspired by the north of our country. Special thanks to the late, great Zosali-Naa Chief Thomas Tia Sulemana and his family, particularly Ma Mariama, Anatu, and Afishetu. I am indebted to Wedadu Sayibu not only for being a great source of inspiration but also for her translation of phrases into Dagbanli. For assistance with Gonja, I thank Rafa Adam.

For translations into Twi and a beady eye on my Ghanaian pidgin, I thank Nana Asaase, Kwabena Opoku-Agyemang, and Kobina Ankomah-Graham; for consultations about Ga, Nii Ayikwei Parkes; and for help with Nigerian pidgin and music rights advice, Chuma Nwokolo.

The opening lines of the beautiful song "No One Like You," by P-Square (the owners of the copyright), are referenced with my thanks as a superfan.

I am grateful to my countryman, artist Bright Ackwerh, not only for bringing Faiza and Makola to life on the cover of this book, but for the care he took in rendering symbolic patterns throughout the chapters. These are inspired by our rich artistic heritage of textiles—particularly Kente and Adinkra—and of pottery and murals, notably from the artwork of Sirigu in northern Ghana, including the Sirigu Women's Organization of Pottery and Art (SWOPA).

I acknowledge the Burt Award for its generous support of the first publication of this story in Ghana.

I thank John House for getting in touch after he found a copy of it in the US and for doggedly encouraging me to publish it beyond Ghana.

I am most grateful to my sister Rosina for her care of our mother while I worked through the editorial process.

And to my parents—none of it would be possible without the abundance of your love, support, and pride in me.

MAMLE WOLO

is an award-winning Ghanaian-German author who studied at the University of Cambridge and Lancaster University in the UK and is an Honorary Fellow in Writing of the University of Iowa. She is a director of the Writers Project of Ghana. She writes fiction, poetry, and screenplays, and lives in Accra, Ghana.